Ain't Nothing Like a

Brooklyn Bitch

By: Kellz Kimberly

Text **KKP** to **22828** for Updates, Spoilers, Giveaways, Announcements, & So Much More!!!!!

Chapter 1

Do you like the way I flick my tongue or nah? You can ride my face until you dripping cum. Can you lick the tip then throat the dick or nah? Can you let me stretch that pussy out or nah? I'm not the type to call you back tomorrow but the way you wrappin 'round me is a problem. Ain't nobody tryna save ya baby, get that paper.

The song was blaring through the speakers as I shook my ass. I made each cheek bounce, which made the crowd go wild. I spun around the pole a couple of times and ended in my signature move. Whenever I did this move the crowd went wild. I climbed all the way to the top, started walking on the ceiling, did a flip in the air and then landed in a split. Just as I expected, the crowd started cheering and throwing bills on the stage. After gathering my money, I went back to the dressing room. I was done for the night. I wasn't in to the private and table dances. I only liked to perform on stage, that way these perverts couldn't rub all over me. The other strippers thought I was stuck up, but I wasn't, I just didn't want these old ass men touching me.

Chix on Dix was not your average strip joint. It was this run down hole in the wall place over in Cypress Hill. Only old dudes that couldn't get laid came here, but I couldn't complain because they paid well and it was putting clothes on me and my sister's back and food in our mouths. Stripping is not how I imaged my life, but at 17 I did what I had to do in order to take care of my 9-year- old sister.

Paige and I were all we had. Our father was nowhere to be found and our mom was a figment of our imagination. She never stayed around too long; she was always on the move. She always told me that I ruined her life and if it wasn't for me she would be someone important. No one told her to open her legs to every Tom, Dick and Harry around. That was probably where she was now, somewhere with her legs spread or downing a bottle of liquor. I pushed the thoughts of my mother out of my head so I could hurry and get home to my sister.

I changed my clothes and was out the door before anyone could stop me and try to get me to stay. It was a hot summer night and the buses were running extra slow. I must have been standing at the bus stop for over an hour and there was still no bus. I was tired of using public transportation, I needed to get a car and quick. I was about to walk the 8 blocks to the train station when a black Audi pulled up to the bus stop. There were a lot of creeps in this neighbourhood so I reached in my bag for my mace. The passenger window rolled down and the prettiest grey eyes were staring at me. I started to feel uncomfortable and nervous so I got up and started walking.

"Hold up ma, do you need a ride?," the stranger asked.

"No, I'm okay I'm just going to walk to the train station," I answered, sounding nervous. I was gripping the can of mace so tight my hand was turning red.

"You shouldn't be walking around at this time of night," he said.

"The train station is not that far, I'll be okay."

"Ma, who you kidding? The train station is like 9 blocks from here!"

"Look, I don't even know you to be getting in your car in the first place. Like I said, I will be okay, but thanks for the offer," I shot back and started walking at a quicker pace. This nigga must have thought I was crazy to get in the car with a complete stranger.

I walked about a block before I heard someone jogging behind me. I turned around so fast with my can of mace drawn you would have thought I had a gun. I was shocked to see that it was the guy from the car.

"Ma, hold up don't kill me now," he laughed.

"I wasn't going to kill you, I was going to blind your ass. What are you doing running up behind me anyway?"

"I already told you, you shouldn't be walking this late out here by yourself so I'm gonna walk with you." I was shocked as hell. Why would a guy get out of a car to walk with a complete stranger in this hot, humid weather?

"I would tell you that you don't have to do that but I can tell you're very persistent."

"That I am. So Miss....."

"Royal." I told him. He wasn't getting any other answers from me besides my name. I figured that was the least I could give him since he was walking me to the train station.

"Royal, hmm, it's different. What is a young lady like you doing walking out here this late?"

"Not to be rude, but I'm not really in the mood to talk. I just wanna get home. " I really wasn't trying to be rude. I just didn't know this guy from a hole in the wall. What I look like telling him my whole life story? I wasn't one of those chicks that jumped all over a guy; especially one that I felt was trying to save me. I didn't need saving, I was doing just fine. The rest of the walk was kind of awkward. I couldn't have been happier when we made it to the train station.

"Well thanks for walking me," I mumbled.

"No problem," he smiled as he walked away and jumped back in the black Audi. I shrugged my shoulders and went to swipe my metro card so I could get on the train. I ended up falling asleep for the entire train ride.

When I got home checked on Paige. She was sound asleep in her Hello Kitty bed. She looked so peaceful laying there sleeping, I went over and kissed her on the cheek. Paige was my heart and everything I did, I did for her. She would never have to want or need for anything as long as I was living and breathing.

I went to my room and stripped out of my clothes so I could take a shower. It was already 4:00 in the morning. All I wanted to do was wash my ass and get a few hours of sleep before I had to get up to get Paige ready for camp. When I got out the shower I dried off, lotioned my body with coco- butter and layed down. The life I lived was a stressful one, but as long as Paige had a smile on her face then I would carry the weight of the world on my shoulders.

******

"Wake up Royal, I'm gonna be late!" Paige said, causing me to jump up. I turned and looked at the clock. It read 9:45. I had 15-minutes to get her to camp. Lucky for me, Paige was already dressed.

"Come on so I can make you breakfast and then I'll get dressed."

I made her a bowl of cereal with fruit on the side. I didn't have time to make her anything else. I ran upstairs and threw on a shirt and some shorts. I washed my face, brushed my teeth and combed my hair out before throwing it into a ponytail. I didn't have to worry about Paige's hair because I always kept it braided. When I came back downstairs she was done with breakfast and standing by the front door with her bag.

"You got everything? " I asked her.

"Yup, now let's go."

Her school was only 10 minutes away so she wouldn't be too late. It wasn't too hot outside so I enjoyed the walk. I loved walking Paige to camp every morning, it gave us a chance to just talk.

"Royal, can we go out to eat when you come to pick me up?" Paige asked once we made it to her school.

"Yes we can, as long as you behave today," I answered.

"Okay. I love you Royal!" she said, giving me a hug and running into the school.

"I love you too," I replied, even though she was already gone.

I started walking back home I didn't have work tonight so I was free for the day. Unlike most 17-year-olds, I didn't chill out and go clubbing. I was more of a home body. I'd rather stay in the house, cook and watch a movie than go out to the club, which is how I graduated high school a year early. I was always at home studying and reading and I pushed myself to get good grades. I planned on going to a community college or a four-year college in the fall if everything worked out. I didn't want to be a stripper forever, I had different goals I wanted to achieve.

"Royal!" Someone called out, pulling me out of my thoughts.

"Yea Aria," I muttered, walking towards the black BMW.

"I'm your mother, you better show me some respect!" she snapped, getting out the car.

"Okay mother." I wasn't really interested in what she had to say. If I truly didn't give a fuck I would tell her ass off, but like she said, she is my mother.

"That's better. I just came from the house. I left you and Paige a little something, it's on your dresser. Matter of fact, where is Paige?" she had the nerve to ask.

"She's at camp."

"Oh yea I forgot. I'll be back later, I'm about to go to Atlantic City with Mark."

"Okay. Well, I have stuff to do so bye."

"Don't be fucking these little boys out here Royal. When I'm gone you're supposed to look out for your sister."

"I'm not you," I mumbled under my breath.

"Don't get smart now!" she replied, getting in the car and leaving.

I didn't understand how a mother could leave their children and chase after some dick. When I got home I checked to see how much money she left us. She had the nerve to leave $30. All I could do was shake my head. I wasn't going to let my mother's bullshit mess up my day; it was only eleven o'clock so I still had time to clean before I had to pick up Paige. I turned on my stereo and started cleaning. I was in the zone when I felt my phone vibrating in my pocket. I ran and turned the music down before I answered.

"Hello."

"Wassup, girl what you doing?" My best friend Justice asked.

"Nothing, cleaning until I have to go get Paige and then I'm taking her out to eat."

"I know you don't work tonight so come out with me," she begged.

"Nah, I wanna spend some time with Paige."

"You always spend time with Paige! She can stay here and play with my sister."

"I don't know, I'll let you know later if I'm coming or not," I told her.

"I don't even know why you're frontin' cause you know you're coming so pack a bag for both you and Paige," she laughed and hung up the phone.

Justice was wild, she was the complete opposite of me. All she did was party and get turnt up. Don't get me wrong, Justice was smart. She graduated early like I did, she just wasn't into the school stuff so instead of going to college, she just stayed home. I really didn't wanna go out and leave Paige but I already knew Justice was gonna drag me out with her. I finished cleaning and packed our overnight bags. By the time I was done it was time to go pick up my mini- me

Chapter 2

"So what are we doing tonight?" Paige asked as we were walking out of Applebee's.

"What do you mean what are we doing?" I chuckled. Sometimes Paige was to grown for her own good.

"What are we gonna do when we get home? I don't have camp tomorrow let's stay up late," she suggested.

"I was gonna let you stay the night with Macy."

"Really? I miss her. I haven't seen her in a while," she smiled.

We hopped on the train and headed over to Justice's house. During the train ride, Paige told me about how camp went. We were having a good convo until she brought up our mother.

"When is ma coming back?" she asked.

I didn't know what to say. How do you tell an 9-year- old that their mother would rather chase after dick instead of being with her kids?

"She came by today. She said she loves you and she left you this," I answered, pulling out a gold locket that had one of the only pictures of her and our mother inside of it. I brought it for Paige about 3 months ago. I planned to give it to her when she finished camp, but after seeing my mother and her leaving again, I decided to give it to her today.

"It's so pretty, did she bring you one?" she asked.

"No she didn't, she wanted you to have it because you are special," I told her.

"Don't worry Royal, I think you're special too, we can share mine."

I smiled at her while I helped her put it on. When we got off the train, we hopped in a dollar cab because I was not in the mood to walk the eleven blocks to Justice's house. The cab pulled up to her house in less than 10 minutes. I paid the guy and we got out. I guess she saw us get out the cab, because before I could even knock, the door swung open.

"Bout time y'all got here. Hey Paige, Macy is in her room," she said, letting us in. As soon as Paige gave Justice her overnight bag, she was ghost. Justice and I laughed at her. When she and Macy got together, it was double trouble.

"Where is your mom?" I asked Justice as we sat in the living room.

"She went away for the weekend so we got the house to ourselves."

Justice's mom wasn't around too often either, but she always made sure Justice and Macy were taken care of.

"Oh 'ight, so where are we going anyway?" I asked.

"We goin' to Lowkey Lounge tonight," she announced.

"It better not be ratchet either, you know I'm not mixy," I warned her.

"Don't worry about it you're gonna have fun!" she laughed.

"Whatever bitch. But tell me why when I was waiting for the bus last night a car pulled up next to me and the dude inside was like, get in I'll give you a ride."

"I know your ass didn't get in that car."

"I didn't. I told him no thank you and started walking. Next thing I know, the dude was jogging up behind me so that he could walk with me."

"Damnnnn! Did you at least get his number?"

"Nah, I just said thank you and got on the train."

"You a dumb bitch, I would have got his number. Who do you know from the hood that is going to get out of a car to walk a stranger to the train station?"

"Bitch I'm not dumb, I was just trying to get home. I didn't have time for a social call."

"That's what you always say. Since I'm taking you out you should cook us something to eat."

"Paige and I already ate."

"Yea, but Macy and I didn't and the baby sitter doesn't know how to cook."

"'Ight I'll cook, only because I don't want Macy and Paige to starve. I could care less about your ass eating," I told her as I went in the kitchen.

Justice's house always had food in it, so it wasn't hard to find something I would be able to cook quickly. I took out the stuff I needed to make spaghetti with a salad on the side. It wasn't anything fancy but it would do. When I finished cooking, I made Macy a plate and called her down to the kitchen. When she came, Paige was right behind her.

"Macy come eat your food," I told her.

"Where's mine?" my sister asked.

"I didn't think you were hungry because we just ate."

"I just want salad then," she said, pulling out a chair and sitting at the table.

"Where's my plate at?" Justice asked, walking into the kitchen fully dressed to go to the club.

"You can make your own plate, I am not your maid. I'm about to go upstairs and get ready."

While I was in the shower, I was trying to figure out what I was going to wear. I didn't really have party clothes because I was never the partying type, but I figured I would just go through Justice's closet because she always had some shit in there. When I got out of the shower I looked through all her stuff. Justice was my bitch, but she wore a lot of revealing things that I really wasn't up for wearing. I decided I would wear my leather jogger pants that I brought with me. I pulled out a crop top from Justice's closet that had the words 'Caution' on it and I threw on a pair of her black pumps. After getting dressed, I looked at myself in the mirror.

There was nothing really special about the outfit I had on, but my self-confidence is what set me apart from the chicks that were gonna be in the club trying to stunt with their $1,200 dresses.

If there was one thing my mom blessed me with, it was my looks. I was 5'7 with a nice slender frame, I had b- cup breasts that were just enough for a handful and I was thick on the bottom. Not that crazy type of thick, but I had enough thighs and ass for someone my size. My skin was a mocha complexion and I had nice shoulder length hair. Growing up I was teased about my skin complexion, being that I had hazel eyes. I had to learn that everything about me was beautiful, regardless if other people saw it or not. That is why I could step out in a regular outfit and still turn heads because my self-confidence spoke volumes. After getting dressed and putting curls in my hair, I was ready to go. When I went back to the living room Justice was talking to the baby sitter while Macy and Paige were watching a movie.

"Look at you mama!" Justice whistled.

"Oh shut up, You ready to go?" I asked her.

"Yea I'm ready to go. Macy make sure you behave yourself, I don't wanna hear nothing bad tonight, okay?"

"Okay," Macy said, getting up and going to give Justice a hug.

I walked over to Paige, gave her a hug and told her I loved her. There was no need for me to tell her to behave because she was a well-behaved kid so I had no worries. We left and hopped in her mother's Mercedes. When we pulled up to the club, the line was around the block. Justice could stand in the line all she wanted, but my ass wasn't gonna do it.

"I hope you know I'm not standing in that long ass line," I told her as we got out the car.

"Do I look like I'm the type of chick that stands in lines?" she stated, walking up to the door.

Going against my better judgment, I followed her to the door. She whispered something to the bouncer at the door before giving him a hug and waving her hand towards me so I could follow her in. I was shocked as hell that we got in but as I got a better look at the bouncer, I saw that it was her cousin. We got inside and it was jammed packed from wall to wall. We found a small table in the back and sat down.

"I need a drink," Justice said.

"We just got here," I told her.

"So what? I'm about to turn up with my niggas Pat & Ron," she giggled.

She waved the waitress over and ordered a shot of Patron and an Long Island tea. I just ordered a coke because I knew I had to be the designated driver. We got our drinks and I started dancing in my seat. I didn't know who the DJ was, but he was going in. As soon as I heard, Nobody Haffi Know by Kranium, I grabbed Justice's hand and we made our way to the dance floor. I was whining and grinding my hips like my life depended on it. Once the song was over, I made my way back over to the table. Justice went over to the bar to get another drink and said she would meet me over there.

I had to push my way through everyone just to get to my table, only to see that it had been taken by some chick and her nigga.

"Excuse me but this is my table," I informed them.

"I don't see your name on it," The chick had the nerve to say.

"You don't have to see my name, I'm telling you it's my table," I told her again.

"What's your name ma?" The dude asked.

"My name is, this is my table!" I answered with attitude.

"You really just gonna flirt with this bitch in my face?" the girl snapped.

"What's going on over here?" Justice asked, walking up to the table.

"Nothing, I was gonna tell your friend here that I have a VIP table that she is more than welcome to have," the dude answered.

"Shit, let's go then!" Justice said, sounding a little too eager.

Him saying that annoyed me because if this nigga had a table in VIP, what the fuck was he doing down here? We followed him upstairs to the VIP section and he led us to the table that was now ours.

"Y'all can have the table for the rest of the night. I'll even send a bottle up for you girls," he offered.

"Thank you," I said, trying to be polite after he pissed me off.

We partied the rest of the night and I truly enjoyed myself. Once the club let out everyone was in the parking lot. Justice's ass was too drunk to do anything. I had to hold her up until we made it to the car. As we walked closer to the car, the dude from inside the club was sitting on the hood of our car. I put Justice in the passenger seat and tried to walk around to the driver side, but dude walked in my path.

"Where you going ma, don't act like you don't see me standing here," he said, licking his lips as if he was LL Cool J.

"I'm just trying to get home," I answered.

"You always trying to get home!" he laughed.

"What are you talking about?" I asked, confused.

"You don't remember me do you?" he smiled.

I took a better look at him and he was definitely handsome. He looked to be about 6'5, his skin was a beautiful caramel complexion and he had some pretty grey eyes. However, after staring at him, I still had no clue who he was.

"No, I don't."

"That's crazy! I get out my car to walk you to the train station and you don't remember me Royal?"

"Oh shit," I said, a little embarrassed.

"Your ass remembers me now huh? It's all good though Slim," he smiled, showing off his dimples.

"Since you know my name it's only right you tell me yours," I said, trying to make up for the fact that I didn't even remember who he was.

"My name is Pharaoh."

"Pharaoh huh? I like it."

"I don't," he said, looking down and shaking his head.

"Why not? It's different and unique."

"I could be different and unique with a common name."

"Okay, so why don't you like it?"

"Cause my last name is King."

"No, it's not!" I laughed.

"I love my mom, but I don't know what she was thinking."

"It's cute."

"If you say so ma, but I came over here so I could get your number before I got up out of here."

"I don't know about that, I really don't have time for a relationship."

"Who said I wanted a relationship?"

"Oh...." I said, not knowing what else to say.

"Royal pick your face up ma, just put your number in my phone," he joked.

I took his phone out his hand and put my number in. Once I gave it back, he said he would hit me up later. I got in the car ready to get my ass home and go to sleep.

"What was all that about?" Justice slurred.

"Nothing. That was the dude that walked me to the train," I told her, pulling off.

"Oh that was captain save a stripper?" she giggled.

"Shut up with your drunk ass!"

I couldn't stand when Justice would drink, which is why I never really went out with her. Whenever she would get liquor in her system, she would throw in my face that I was a stripper.

"Once he find out what you do for a living he ain't gonna want your ass no more."

"Let's get this shit straight. I'm tired of you throwing this shit in my face. Yea I strip, but I don't do it 'cause I want to, I do it to take care of my little sister bitch."

"Yea, whatever. Like I said, when he find out you shake your ass for a living he's not gonna want you."

I just shook my head because she really had me fucked up. I was trying not to go off because Justice had been my best friend for years. She had a mother that took care of her, and anything else she wanted she got from the niggas she fucked with. She didn't know about struggle, but for her to throw this shit in my face as if I do it just to do it was the last straw. I was tired of hearing the shit.

As soon I pulled up into her driveway, I called a cab. It was four in the morning and I didn't want to wake up Paige, but I for damn sure wasn't gonna stay here either. The cab driver honked his horn letting me know he was outside. I picked Paige up, got our bags and left. I didn't bother telling Justice I was leaving. I didn't even know if she made it out of the car. By the time the cab pulled up to my house the sun was coming up.

"Can you make me breakfast?" Paige asked when we walked in the house.

"Paige, go upstairs and lay down. When you wake up their will be breakfast on the table."

"Okay," she yawned and went upstairs.

I was right behind her because I was beyond tired. I changed my clothes and went to put my phone on the charger when I noticed I had a text message.

Pharaoh

Just making sure you got home alright ma, Hit me when you get up. Goodnight and sweet dreams Royal.

I smiled at the text and climbed into bed. I wasn't sure about how I felt about Pharaoh but after that text, he just gained some points.

Chapter 3

I woke up later that day with my phone going off the hook. I picked it up and saw that I had five missed calls and a text; all from Justice. With the way she acted last night, she damn sure wasn't going to get a phone call from me, but I did decide to read her text.

Justice

Bitch why would you leave me in the fucking car knowing my ass was drunk. You real fucked up for that shit.

I looked at that shit in disbelief , like she really couldn't be serious. I wasn't even going to respond. I threw my phone on the bed and went into the bathroom to brush my teeth and wash my face. After cleaning myself up I went to Paige's room to see what she was up to but she wasn't there. I checked for her in the living room and she was on the couch eating a bowl of cereal and watching cartoons.

"Why didn't you wake me up? I would have cooked you breakfast," I said, sitting down next to her.

"I didn't want to wake you, you looked tired and I like cereal," she shrugged.

"I know you do," I said, laughing at her.

I sat back and watched cartoons with her. I had to work later tonight so I wanted to spend as much time with her as I could. I hated leaving her in the house alone but I had no other choice. I would never leave when she was up, I always waited until she was sleep. Our next-door neighbor had a key to our apartment and she would come and check on Paige from time to time. I was getting tired of stripping, but it was the only way I could provide for us.

We watched cartoons well into the evening, until my mother decided to show her face. She came stumbling into the house smelling like liquor. I already knew it was about to be some drama.

"Mommy!!!" Paige yelled when she saw my mother walk through the door.

"Heyyyyyy babyyyyyy," she slurred back, giving Paige a hug.

"Mommy you stink," Paige said, backing up some.

"I know baby, mommy 'bout to go get in the shower. Royal don't act like you don't see me standing here," she said, turning her head and looking my way.

"Hey Aria," I smirked. Paige hadn't seen her ass in I don't know how long, but when she does decide to bring her ass home she comes home smelling like a damn bottle.

"You keep trying me, I've told you before about that Aria shit," she said, getting in my face.

"Paige go to your room," I said, never taking my eyes off my mother.

Paige looked at the both of us before slowly making her way to her room. I didn't want her to see this and feel like it was okay to disrespect our mother. However, my mother needed to be put in her place and I was just the person to show her right where that place was.

"I don't know why you told her to go to her room, you ain't gonna do shit," my mother said laughing.

"Look, you need to get yourself together or get the fuck out. All you do is chase dick that's not chasing you. Paige hasn't seen you in a minute and when she finally does, you wanna come up in here pissy drunk."

"Don't tell me how to raise my fucking child. I had her not you, and so fucking what if I chase after dick, that's my business. Just remember I brought you into this world Royal and I will take your ass out. I don't know who put a battery in your back, but you need to take that shit out. Got the nerve to tell me to get out of my own house," she slurred, trying to walk past. I moved over to the right, making sure I was blocking her path.

"Royal, you better move the fuck out of my way!" she yelled.

"Ma like I said to you before, it's either you gonna get your shit together or get out. I pay the rent in this house and I am the one that has been taking care of Paige. You can't keep running in and out of her life, that shit isn't healthy for her," I said, trying not to cry. It was sad that I had to have this conversation with my own damn mother.

"Royal, do not tell me what is healthy for my fucking daughter. Did you think it was healthy for me to have you at fucking 16? No! But guess what? I still did it!" she yelled.

Before I could even respond, her open hand landed on the right side of my cheek. I couldn't believe she had just slapped me.

"If you ever disrespect me like that again I will do more than just slap you," she warned and walked past me.

I turned around hot on her heels ready to beat her ass when I saw Paige peeking around the corner. The look on Paige's face was breaking my heart, I watched my mom walk into her room and slam the door.

"Paige come back out here and watch cartoons," I told her.

"Okay, can you watch them with me?" she asked, looking at me with sadness in her eyes.

"Not right now."

"Why did mommy hit you Royal?"

"She was just mad that I told her she had to leave until she got better."

"Where is she going to go?"

"I'm not sure, but as long as you're okay that is all that matters," I said and gave her a hug. I handed her back the remote control and went to my room.

I was beyond pissed off that she put her hands on me, but I still stood by what I said. From the looks of our conversation she wasn't going to change, but she was gonna get the fuck out of here. I needed to make plans to change the locks on the doors as soon as she left. I flopped on the bed and closed my eyes trying to forget everything that had just happened.

Well this has gotta be the longest crush ever. If I ever get to fuck it'd be the longest bust ever. Love is a drug, like the strongest stuff ever, and fuck it I'm on one your feel me? She on a power trip she got me where she want a nigga. Wifin' in the club, man my homies gone' disown a nigaa.

I heard my ringtone playing, but I let the song play out before I picked up my phone to see who was calling me. I didn't recognize the number but decided to call the number back anyway because not a lot of people had my number to begin with. The phone rung about three times before the person picked up.

"Hello? Did somebody call me from this number?" I asked.

"Wassup Slim! I sent you a text last night, you didn't save a nigga's number?" he asked.

I blushed at the sound of his voice. "I knocked out once I got home, but wassup with you?"

"Nothing, just got done handling some business and I wanted to see if you wanted to kick it for a few."

I looked at the clock and it read 5 o'clock. I had more than enough time to kick it with him but I didn't wanna leave Paige in the house, especially with my mother.

"Not today. I have to watch my sister and I have to work later."

"Baby sis can come with us and I'll have you back home by the time you have to be at work."

"I don't know," I hesitated, unsure because I just met him and didn't wanna seem thirsty.

"You acting like I'm trying to marry yo' ass Slim. Just come chill with a nigga," he said laughing.

"Okay, okay. I'ma text you my address, I should be ready in about a half hour."

"Ight Royal, just text that info when you ready," he said and hung up.

I was excited about going out with Pharaoh and the fact that he invited my sister was a plus. I didn't know how far this was going to go or how far I wanted it to go. Yes, I was attracted to him and wouldn't mind dating him, but I came with baggage that I didn't know if he was ready for. The last dude I was with had me thinking I was in love with him but what we had really wasn't love. Once he got what he was looking for he just up and left. I wanted to tell Pharaoh that I wasn't going to be a one night stand but I didn't wanna run him off by saying that either. I figured I would play it safe and not say too much of anything and see how it all played out.

******

I didn't know where we were going but I was enjoying the ride. Pharaoh and Paige were talking up a storm; I was starting to feel a little left out. I was glad those two were vibing though because whomever I chose to talk to they had to get along with Paige. After driving for about twenty minutes we finally pulled up to our destination. We pulled up to a town house that looked like it was built in the late 1800s. The outside was beautiful and I couldn't help but wonder what the inside looked like.

"You just gonna stand there or are you gonna come in?" Pharaoh asked, walking past me with Paige at his side.

"Shut up I'm coming," I shot back.

"Hurry up so I can give y'all a tour of my house," he said.

I grabbed Paige's hand as we followed Pharaoh around the house. I had to admit that I was impressed. His house didn't look like anything I expected it to. Everything looked neat and cleaned, like it had a woman's touch to it. The downstairs where the kitchen and living room were had a black and burgundy color scheme going on that I was in love with, because burgundy and black were my favorite colors. Upstairs had a grey and white color scheme, a master bedroom with its own bathroom, and another bedroom with an extra half-bath. The house was beautiful, but I was wondering who was living in it with him.

"So what you think?" Pharaoh asked, as we all sat down in the living room.

"I like it!" Paige said, smiling.

"I'm glad you like it Paige. Here, take the remote and watch TV while me and Royal go in the kitchen and talk."

"Okay," she said, turning the T.V on.

Once we got in the kitchen, he went in the fridge, grabbed two bottles of water and passed one to me.

"Thank you, your house is beautiful by the way. You live here alone?"

"Come on Slim, say what you got to say. Don't sugar coat shit."

"I'm not sugar coating anything."

"Yea 'ight, but yea, I live here alone. My moms helped me decorate though, I just picked out the colors and footed the bill," he laughed, causing his dimples to show.

"Well then your mom did a great job."

"She did huh? But enough about the house," he said, moving closer to me, invading my personal space.

"Then what do you wanna talk about?" I asked, staring at those gray eyes that I knew I could grow to love. Those eyes of his had to make a couple of females wanna give it up because they were making my panties wet.

"I wanna talk about us. I want you Slim," he expressed.

"How can you want someone you just met? I'm sure you want a lot of women and those same women want you."

"I'm not gonna lie, you're right, I do want a lot of women. Beyoncé is number one on that list and you're number two," he grinned and moved back toward me.

"I could never be number two. Once you fuck with me you will be craving me and I'm not talking in a sexual way either," I told him, leaning in and seductively licking my lips.

"What that mouth do though?" he said with a lustful gaze in his eyes.

"You will never know," I said laughing.

Paige was too quiet so I went to go check on her. Walking in the living room, I saw Paige knocked out with the remote still in her hand.

"You can lay her down in the guest room," Pharaoh said, sneaking up on me.

"Nah that's okay, we should be getting home. I have to get ready to go to work anyway."

"It's cool Slim, she can sleep here and when you get off just come here to get her and I'll bring y'all home."

I thought about what he said and it made sense but at the same time, I had just met dude. Did I really trust him enough to let him watch my sister?

"Look I'm not going to hurt her 'ight, so you might as well just leave her here," he said, picking her up and bringing her upstairs.

I grabbed my phone out my bag to call a cab service so I could get to work. I damn sure didn't want him trying to bring me to work. As soon as I was hanging up the phone, Pharaoh was coming downstairs.

"Who was that?" he asked, sitting next to me.

"You haven't even got a sample of me yet and you already asking who I'm talking to," I giggled.

"I'm not jacking you or anything I just don't wanna be disrespected in my house." The look on his face let me know that nothing was funny and he was very serious.

"I would never disrespect you, but I was calling a cab to take me to work."

"I could have taken you Slim."

"How, when you got my sister upstairs?" I asked, looking at him as if he was crazy.

"You right Slim, but wassup? I'm trying to see you."

"I have way too much going on right now and I'm sure you don't need any baggage."

"Everyone has baggage ma, now tell me what's up."

"I need to move out and get my own place so I don't have to deal with my fucked up mother. I want to go to school but can't find time because I take care of Paige. To top it all off, I'm tired of shaking my damn ass at Chix & Dix."

As soon as that last part came out, I made an "oh shit" face. I didn't mean for that part to come out but it was one of many things wrong in my life. At the same time, I thought back to what Justice said. *When he find out what you do for a living he ain't gonna want your ass anymore.* She kind of had a point, but at least he found out before we took this any further.

"Hold up, you work at Chix & Dix?" he asked, screwing up his face.

"Yea and you don't even have to say anything, because the look on your face says it all!" I said, getting up and going upstairs to get Paige.

From the look on his face, I knew he didn't like the idea of me stripping, but it really didn't matter what he liked because it was putting food on the table for me and my sister.

"Paige get up!" I yelled, shaking her.

"I'm tired Royal," she mumbled, turning over.

"Come on, we have to go home," I told her, pulling her up.

I helped her put her sneakers on and damn near carried her downstairs. Pharaoh was still in the same spot that I left him in. I looked at him and sucked my teeth before I grabbed my bag and tried to make my way to the door. I guess Pharaoh was over the shock because he snatched the bag out my hand.

"Yo, bring baby sis back upstairs," he said, adding some bass to his voice.

"Nah, we about to go home, the cab should be here by now."

"Royal, what the fuck did I just say! Bring her back up stairs and then get your ass back on this couch!" I had to do a double take to make sure it was him talking.

"Paige, go upstairs until I tell you that the cab is here," I told her, putting her down.

Once I knew she was out of earshot I turned towards Pharaoh like he had lost his damn mind.

"I don't know what kind of bitches you been fucking with but I'm not one of them. Don't fucking talk to me like that!" I yelled. If it was one thing I hated it was someone telling me what to do. My own mother didn't even boss me around and I'll be damn if I let this nigga do it.

"Look at you trying to boss up!" he laughed.

If looks could kill this nigga would have been dead, he just tried to chastise me like I was a child and now he was laughing at me.

"I don't find anything funny, oh but look at that, the cab is right on time," I told him, showing him my vibrating phone.

He took the phone out my hand and told the cab driver the cab was no longer needed. Pharaoh was really starting to work my damn nerves; he wasn't my man so I didn't need him telling me what to do.

"Royal fix your face, I didn't mean to get loud with you but you a hot head and you're stubborn as fuck," he said laughing.

"How am I a hot head? The look on your face when I accidently told you where I worked said everything that needed to be said. Plus, I don't know why you told dude I didn't need that cab because I still need to get to work." I wasn't gonna touch on the fact that he called me stubborn because he was on point with that one.

"Slim, your ass isn't going to work today, tomorrow or ever. You no longer work at Chix & Dix." He smirked at me.

"Pharaoh you can't tell me where I can and can't work, you're not my man," I replied, getting annoyed.

"I'm not trying to be your man, I'm trying to be a friend. You said you didn't wanna work there anymore so now you don't have to. Simple," he added, like it was really that simple.

"Then where am I going to work? You know I still have to support myself and Paige and I'm not going to take money from you if that's what you're thinking."

"Chill out Royal damn, my mom runs a hair salon for me. You can work there."

"Why are you trying to help me Pharaoh? You don't even know me." I wanted to make sure his intentions were pure because if he was looking for something in return then he was gonna be in for a rude awakening.

"I know everything I need to know Slim. When I rolled up on you in an Audi you didn't seem impressed at all. Shit, you tried to mace my ass," he laughed.

"You would have been maced too, but I didn't wanna mess up those pretty eyes," I grinned.

"The point is Slim, any other chick would have jumped in the car just because it was an Audi. You different ma and that's hard to find nowadays. Everything you're doing you're doing it because you're trying to better yourself for you and baby sis, so how could I not want to help you out."

"Okay, Okay, I guess you have a point, but I'm about to go upstairs and check on Paige," I said smiling. Since I wasn't going to work then I was about to take my ass to sleep.

"Ight Slim, good night," he said, smiling at me before picking up the remote and turning on the TV.

I walked up the stairs blushing with the biggest smile on my face. I still wanted to be friends with Pharaoh, but if he played his cards right this nigga could have my last name.

Chapter 4

This last month has been crazy! The day after I spent the night at Pharaoh's house I started working at the salon. His mom was real cool, but I couldn't say the same thing for the other chicks in there. I'm not sure why but this one chick Bia kept coming for me. I didn't know what her problem was but if she kept up the bullshit I was gonna solve it for her. I did become cool with this chick named Emerie. She was a cool, laid-back chick. She was 19 so we were close in age, which was probably the reason we clicked. As far as Pharaoh and I went, he would come into the shop and flirt with me from time to time but I had to let him know that we were nothing more than friends.

Today Paige and I were going to go apartment hunting because I just couldn't live with my mother anymore. I tried changing the locks once she left but she had some nigga that I assumed was Mark, come in and kick the shit in. After that I knew that the only way I was going to be able to have a peace of mind was by moving out and the sooner I did that the better.

"Paige come on, Pharaoh's outside," I yelled.

"Okay I'm coming," she said, rushing out of the bedroom.

I grabbed my bag and shut what was left of our front door. Walking towards Pharaoh's car I noticed that somebody was in the front seat. Getting a better look at the person, I noticed it was Bia. I rolled my eyes, helped Paige into the back seat and buckled her in.

"Wassup baby sis?" Pharaoh greeted Paige as he pulled off.

"Hey Pharaoh," she spoke, smiling. When she got around Pharaoh she had the biggest smile on her face.

"Wassup Royal?" he asked, looking at me in the rear view mirror.

"Hi," I answered dryly.

I was pissed off because I didn't like Bia and didn't know why she was here to begin with. Plus, I didn't like the fact that her and Pharaoh were spending time together.

"Hey Royal sweetie," Bia said, with a hint of sarcasm in her voice.

"Bia, don't call me sweetie because I'm not a child."

"I'm not saying you're a child, I'm just calling you sweetie since you are younger than me and Pharaoh."

"I guess. You do look like you're pushing thirty so I can understand why you're calling me sweetie."

"Little girl you better watch your mouth!" she said, turning around in her seat to face me.

"Yo, chill with all that dumb shit 'ight!" Pharaoh interrupted.

I sucked my teeth and rolled my eyes because if this bitch would have never come we wouldn't be going through this shit now. I remained silent the entire ride to the first house that we were going to look at. I had no words for Pharaoh. Ever since I told him that I just wanted to be friends he had been acting funny, but bringing Bia along was the ultimate straw. If Bia said one more disrespectful thing out of her mouth then both she and Pharaoh were going to get it. I couldn't believe she had the nerve to try to throw shade because I was younger than Pharaoh. The nigga was only 21.

"Yo Slim, we here," Pharaoh announced, knocking on the back door window.

I was too busy cursing Pharaoh out in my head that I didn't even notice we pulled up to the place. The apartment was out in Williamsburg. It wasn't anything expensive and glamorous, but it was a nice two-bedroom apartment that Paige and I would be comfortable living in.

"I'll take it," I said after we walked through the whole house.

"Humph," Bia grunted, looking around with a disgusted look on her face.

"What are you making noise for Bia? No one asked for your opinion," I responded, ready to slap fire out her mouth.

"I'm just saying I could never live here," she said as she started to walk out the door.

I was more than ready to follow behind her, grab her by her hair, and pull her back in this apartment so I could fuck her up.

"Yo Slim, calm down ma," Pharaoh interrupted, finally stepping in.

"Don't tell me to calm down when you're the one that brought her ass knowing I don't like her. Why are you chilling with her anyway?"

"First off, I didn't know you didn't like her, if I would've known I would have never brought her. Second, why does it matter why I'm chilling with her? I could have sworn you said that we are just friends so don't go acting jealous now," he reminded me, giving me that smirk he gave whenever he made a point.

"Whatever, just tell me when I have to sign the lease and when I can move in. After that you don't have to say anything else to me," I said, grabbed Paige's hand and went to the car. Pharaoh came out of the building maybe five minutes after us with papers in his hands.

"Here, this is your lease. All you have to do is sign it and give it to me," he said once he got in the car.

Reaching in my bag, I pulled out the pen, signed the dotted line and handed him back the lease. He looked over it and handed me a set of keys. I was smiling on the inside about me having my own apartment, but I was still pissed off over everything that happened. Unlike the ride to the apartment, the ride to the salon was not quiet. Bia was talking up a storm about shit that neither Pharaoh nor I cared about. As soon as we got to the salon, I jumped out with Paige and went right into Ms. King's office.

"Hey baby how did the apartment hunting go? Did you find something for you and Paige?" she asked, picking up Paige and putting her on her lap.

"Ms. King, Paige is too big to be sitting on your lap, put her down."

"Girl leave her alone she's not bothering nobody. Now did you find an apartment?"

"Yes I found one. It's all the way out in Williamsburg though, I'ma have to switch Paige's school so she doesn't have to travel too far."

"That's great baby. I know I just met you not to long ago but I am so proud of you and you have done a wonderful job with Paige."

"Thanks Ms. King," I smiled.

"No thanks needed. Now, where is my son?"

"Outside with Bia," I said, rolling my eyes.

"Y'all two are a mess"

"It's not me, it's your son."

"Chile please, you like my son and I know my son likes you. Anybody with eyes can see the chemistry between the two of y'all," she chuckled.

"I have no idea what you're talking about. I'm about to go sit at the front desk, do you mind if I leave Paige back here?"

"You know I don't mind honey," Mrs. King said.

I went back to the front of the shop and sat at the desk. Pharaoh and Bia were out front talking and she kept running her hand over his chest. The sight was making me sick to my stomach and I guess my face showed that because Emerie walked over to me asking why I was looking like that.

"Royal, fix your face," Emerie said, laughing.

"I don't even know why I'm letting this shit get to me. I don't care for Pharaoh like that and I don't like Bia's old ass anyway," I said laughing.

"Yea that's what your mouth is saying but we all know your heart is saying something different."

"Whatever Emerie. I'ma tell you like I have been telling everyone, I do not want Pharaoh."

"Uh huh, keep saying it until your ass believes it honey," she chuckled again, walking away.

Bia came in the shop with a big ass cheesy smile on her face like she was walking in a beauty pageant. I turned my head, paying her ass no mind and continued to answer the phones and schedule appointments.

"Bia why you smiling like that for?" One of the other stylists asked.

"You know Pharaoh is my man and he always puts a smile on my face," Bia grinned.

"Girl you lucky 'cause he is fine as hell!"

"Don't I know it," Bia laughed, giving the girl a hi-five.

"If y'all don't shut up and stop talking about my son and get back to work. His ass don't want y'all anyway, he's just looking for something to stick his dick in," Ms. King shouted out, sticking her head out the door.

I was trying not to laugh aloud but I couldn't help it because the look on Bia's face was priceless. Ms. King looked to see if anyone had anything to say before she closed her office door. Once it closed, I laughed my ass off.

"I don't know what you're laughing for," Bia said.

"Because you need to pick your face up off that floor before someone steps on it," I said, still laughing at Ms. King.

"Royal I get it, it's okay to be jealous that I have something that you want," Bia smirked.

"Bia what do you have that I could possibly want?" I asked her.

"Pharaoh."

I had to laugh at her because I knew she couldn't be serious.

"You think I'm jealous of you because you have Pharaoh? Girl you are dumber than I thought you were."

"Little girl watch your mouth, and you are jealous, but it's okay you will find someone for you sooner or later."

I didn't even respond to that dumb shit, because I was going to show her exactly how jealous I was that she had Pharaoh.

******

It was around nine and the shop was closing. I called Pharaoh earlier and told him I needed a ride to my mother's house. Ms. King had left earlier than usual leaving me, Emerie and Bia to close up.

As we were walking out of the shop, Pharaoh pulled up in front and of course, Bia ran over to him.

"Look at her looking thirsty as ever," Emerie said.

"Don't worry, I'm about to give her ass a bottle of water," I said, walking over to the car and putting Paige in the back seat. I walked over to the passenger's side, jumped in and gave Pharaoh a kiss on the cheek.

"Thank you for picking me up," I told him.

"No problem Slim, you know I got you," he responded, smiling at me.

"You came to get *her?*" Bia asked, looking confused.

"Yea," Pharaoh answered, keeping it short.

"Well, when you're done dropping her off can you come over my place?" Bia asked, sounding more desperate than she looked.

"Nah, I got some shit I have to handle tonight," he said and started to pull off. I stuck my hand out the window and waved goodbye to Emerie who was laughing her ass off.

"Why you lie to that girl, you know you don't have shit to do tonight," I told him, laughing a little.

"Nah, I do I have to handle some business," he told me.

"What business is that?" I asked, trying to be nosey. Ever since I met Pharaoh, he never really talked about what he did for a living.

"You sure you want to know what I do for a living?"

"I probably already know," I sighed.

"Then what I do Slim?" He turned to look at me.

"All I know is that it involves drugs," I said in a hushed tone so Paige didn't hear me.

"And that's all you need to know."

I left the conversation at that because he was right. He wasn't my man so I really didn't need to know what type of business he was in. The way I felt, the less I knew the better. We pulled up to my mom's apartment and I got out the car. Paige fell asleep and I couldn't carry her so Pharaoh decided to carry her. As we got off the elevator, there were clothes all over the hallway.

"The fuck?" I said, picking up the clothes, realizing they were mine.

"What's wrong?" Pharaoh asked, sounding concerned.

I didn't even respond to him. I rushed to my house and found my mother throwing my shit out the door.

"Aria, what are you doing" I yelled, pushing her back in the house.

"I want you to get the fuck out; I'm tired of your shit!" she yelled.

"Aria what are you talking about? I'm barely here and when I am here I'm in my room!" I yelled back, truly confused.

"I don't have to explain shit to you. Just get the rest of your shit and get the fuck up out of my house and who is that holding my fucking daughter?"

"Don't worry about who that is, if you want me to leave fine, but Paige is coming with me!" I told her.

"Paige isn't going anywhere, that is my fucking child!"

"Like I said, Paige is coming with me," I told her, getting in her face. Her eyes were blood shot red, which told me she had been drinking.

"Pharaoh, take Paige back down to the car please while I grab some stuff." I said and pushed past my mother to pack some of Paige's things. I filled up two bags of Paige's stuff and grabbed what I could of mine. When I came back out from my room, my mom was standing by the door blocking it.

"Aria move," I said in a calm tone.

"I'm not moving anywhere unless you're going to call that nigga to bring my daughter back upstairs."

"Aria, I don't want to hurt you but I will if you don't fucking move. I don't know what makes you think I'm going to leave my sister here with your drunk, dick loving ass."

"Royal I told you about that...." Before she could finish I sent a right hook to her face, dropping her instantly. I didn't want to put my hands on her, but she was pissing me off. First she wants to throw my shit into the hallway, and now she wants to block the fucking door. I stepped over her and made my way downstairs to

Pharaoh's car. I threw our bags in the trunk and jumped in the passenger seat.

"You 'ight Royal?" Pharaoh asked me when he pulled off.

"I'm fine, just take me to my new apartment."

"How you and baby sis gonna stay there when you don't even have any furniture? Y'all can stay at my crib until the apartment is fully ready."

I honestly didn't care where I went at this moment, I just didn't wanna be at the house anymore. Aria needed some real help and if she wasn't going to get it then she would leave me no choice but to keep her away from Paige. To make matters worse, I didn't know how I was going to explain everything that happened to Paige but just like everything else, I would find a way. It felt like I was carrying the weight of the world on my shoulders and I didn't know how much longer I was going to be able to keep it up.

Chapter 5

I woke up the next morning to the sun shining in my eyes. I had to adjust my eyesight because the room I was in didn't look familiar. Once my eyes adjusted, I realized I was in Pharaoh's room, but Pharaoh wasn't with me. I got up and went into the guest bedroom to make sure Paige was in there. Peeking in I saw her laid across the bed. I left out the room because I didn't want to wake her.

I went downstairs to see if I could find something to eat when I saw Pharaoh passed out on the couch. The AC was blasting down here. I figured he was cold and ran back upstairs to grab his blanket off the bed. I put it over him and went into the kitchen to look in his fridge. To my surprise it was stocked with food. Since he opened his house up to me the least I could do was make him some breakfast. I took out everything I needed so I could make French toast, cheese eggs and sausage.

I was cleaning up the mess I made when Paige came down stairs rubbing her eyes. She pulled out a chair at the table and sat down while I made her a plate of food. I decided that now would be a good time to explain to her that she wouldn't be seeing Aria for a while.

"Good morning Paige, how did you sleep?" I asked her, putting her plate in front of her.

"I slept great, but why are we here? Can't we go to our new house with mommy?" she asked, taking a bite of French toast.

"We are going to go to the new house as soon as I buy some furniture but mom is not coming."

"Why not Royal?"

"Because she is not ready to take care of you, so until she gets better it's just going to be me and you, okay?"

"Okay Royal, can Pharaoh come with us too?"

"He can come to visit."

"Yay, I like Pharaoh," she smiled.

"I bet you do, now finish your food while I go and take a shower."

"Okay."

"I love you Paige," I told her before I got up.

"I love you too," she said.

I was glad she didn't ask too many questions, I just hoped that when she got older she understood that everything I was doing I was doing it for her. I didn't want to wake up Pharaoh so I searched the house for a towel and a cloth. It didn't take me long to find and once I found everything I got in the shower, hoping to wash some of my stress away.

******

When I got out the shower, I threw back on my clothes and realized I hadn't talked to Justice in over a month. This has been the longest we had ever stopped talking. Even though I didn't like what she said, I felt like I had to be the one to mend our broken friendship. I picked up my phone and dialed her number. After four rings I was going to hang up and say fuck it but she picked up.

"Hello," she answered, acting like she didn't know who it was.

"Wassup?"

"Royal?"

"Justice don't act funny, you know it's me."

"Whatever, what you want though? I haven't talked to you since you left me in the fucking car."

"You act like you didn't deserve it. That whole night you kept throwing in my face how I was stripper, so you damn right I left your drunken ass in the car. But we can both get over that and move on or your ass can stay mad, the choice is yours." I didn't have a problem letting Justice go as a friend. Yes, she is my best friend and I would miss her, but I wasn't in the profession of keeping a friend who didn't want to be a friend.

"Shut up with ya emotional ass, you know damn well I'm not letting your ass go. You stuck with me for life. But what you been up to? I saw you yesterday leaving out with bags of shit."

"Yea I moved out. My moms was wilding and it wasn't good for Paige so I got us our own place."

"Look at you. That stripper money must be coming in good," she teased, laughing.

"Didn't I just tell you about that stripper shit and for your information, I'm not stripping any more hoe, I work at a hair salon."

"I was playing, calm down! But that's wassup, I'm happy for you for real."

"See that's the Justice I know and love!" I said smiling, happy that I got my friend back.

"Shut up. What you doing later? I wanna chill, I miss your ass."

"I have to work later but you can come through if you want to."

"Just text me the address and what time to come and I'll be there. Are you taking Paige with you?"

"Yea I had to take her out of camp because it's too far for me to drop her off, pick her up and go to work."

"Ight, I'ma bring Macy with me so they can play."

"That's cool, but let me go make sure Paige ain't messing up this dude's house."

"Dude? What dude? Let me find out Royal got a bae," Justice laughed, but I knew she was serious as hell.

"I'll put you on later," I said and hung up the phone. Justice was crazy but she was my bitch for real for real.

When I got back downstairs, Paige was in the living room watching TV while Pharaoh was eating the breakfast I made.

"I hope she didn't wake you up," I said, taking a seat on the love seat he had in the corner of the living room.

"Nah it's all good, but good looks with the blanket 'cause a nigga was cold. I was just too tired to get up and get one," he laughed.

"Lazy, but uh what are you doing today?"

"I'm free today. Why wassup, you wanna chill with a nigga?" he smiled, showing off his dimples.

"No I have to go to work and I need a ride."

"I got you ma, you taking baby sis with you today?"

"Yea I don't have a baby sitter, so I have no choice."

"My mom's don't work today why don't you let her watch her?"

"Your mom has done enough. I can't ask her to watch Paige too."

"She don't mind trust me, that lady lives for taking care of people."

"If you ask her and she says yea then I'll let Paige go over there."

"Ight but go put baby sis in the tub, I wanna talk to you on some serious shit."

"Come on Paige so you can wash up and get ready," I said, taking her hand. I ran her some bath water and put some of her bubble bath in there before helping her in.

"If you need me just yell, okay?" I told her. She nodded her head yes and I went back downstairs. As I walked into the living room, Pharaoh was coming out the kitchen talking on the phone. I flipped through the channels trying not to be all in his conversation. After about five minutes, he got off the phone, took the remote out my hand and sat down across from me.

"My mom said she'll watch Paige for you," he said, looking me straight in the eye.

"Okay that's great, but what did you want to talk about?" I asked, feeling kind of nervous.

"Why did you get so mad about me chilling with Bia?"

"Because I don't like her ass. You can chill with her all you want, just don't bring me along when you are doing it."

"Wrong answer, try again."

"What you mean wrong answer? There is no right or wrong answer, there is only the truth and that was it," I said, getting a little annoyed.

"That may be the truth, but it wasn't the whole truth, now keep it a buck with me Slim."

"What do you want me to say, huh? That I like you and I was jealous because she was with you?"

"If it's the truth then yea, that's what I want you to say."

"Fine I like you. I'm feeling you and I was jealous because she was with you and touching all over you because I want you to myself," I admitted, putting my head down, embarrassed that I finally let out the truth.

"Slim pick your head up there is nothing to be embarrassed about."

"How is this supposed to work? I'm 17 and you're 21. Shit, I don't turn 18 until April and that's seven months away."

"Why you doubting a nigga? You may be 17 but your mind set is way beyond that age."

"Whatever. I'm just a kid, this shit will never work."

"Stop doubting yourself. If you want this shit to work it's gonna work. Now you mine and that is the end of it," he announced, getting up and walking up stairs.

How the hell was he going to say that I was his and then just leave the fucking room? I hope I wasn't getting in over my head but on the inside, it felt right. However, my brain was telling me this was the wrong thing to do. All I knew is that he had to let Bia know what was up and quick, because I wasn't going to tolerate no bullshit between those two. If he wanted to be with me then he had to be with only me, and if he wanted to be with her then that was fine too. However, he wasn't going to have the both of us.

When it was time to bring me to work Pharaoh didn't say a word to me, he took Paige's hand and helped her in the car. The entire car ride was silent. I didn't know how this was a great start to our relationship, but if he didn't wanna say anything then neither was I. I sent Justice a text giving her the address and telling her she didn't have to bring Macy with her because I found a baby sitter for Paige. She sent a text back saying she would be there within the hour. Pulling up to the shop, I got out and went towards the backseat to give Paige a hug and tell her that I love her.

"What, I can't get a kiss and a hug?" Pharaoh asked when I turned to walk inside.

"Nope," I answered, looking over my shoulder and going into the shop. I went into the back and dropped my stuff before going to my desk so I could get started. About five minutes after me sitting at my desk, Pharaoh walks in with Paige by his side, comes around my desk, and stands in front of me.

"Where's my kiss Slim?"

"You don't get one since you wanna be acting funny and shit," I said, rolling my eyes.

"Nobody was acting funny, I was just giving you enough time to get your mind right about me and you 'cause I don't wanna hear no more of that doubting shit."

"Yea whatever."

By now, all eyes in the shop were on us and it didn't help that Pharaoh grabbed me by my chin, forcing me to kiss him.

"Call me when you're ready to leave Slim," he said, winking and walking out with Paige.

On the inside, I was smiling like a damn Cheshire cat, but on the outside I had to play it cool for these nosey ass chicks.

"I told you that you wanted him," Emerie laughed, walking past me and slapping me on the ass.

I laughed at her and started answering the phones. I busied myself in my work because I knew as soon as Bia walked in here one of these chicks were going to run their mouth. I wasn't a fighter, but I would beat a bitch ass if I had to. I just hoped it didn't have to come to that.

******

About three hours later Bia strolled in the shop all smiles. I paid her no mind and looked past her because Justice walked in behind her.

"Wassup mama?" Justice asked, giving me a hug.

"Nothing, just chasing that dollar," I responded, pulling up a chair for her.

"I hear that," she laughed.

"Emerie come here," I called out. I wanted to introduce the two because I felt like they would get along.

"Royal you know them bitches are back there telling Bia everything that happened. If shit goes left you know I got your back."

"I'm not worried about them, but Emerie this is my best friend Justice, and Justice, this is Emerie."

"Nice to meet you," Emerie smiled.

"Nice to meet you too, but um Royal, what happened?" Justice asked.

I quickly filled Justice in on everything that happened in the last month up until what happened today with Pharaoh.

"This bitch better not start shit because I'm not the one," Justice said.

"Don't even get all hype, that chick aint gonna do shit!" Emerie piped in.

"She better not," Justice said, rolling her eyes as Bia walked back into the front of the salon.

We continued our conversation, talking about nothing really, when Bia finally got that frog out of her throat and decided to speak to me.

"She so jealous that she just had to go and push up on my nigga. Females can never find their own dick, they always gotta chase after someone else's," Bia said loud enough for the whole shop to hear.

"Bia, Royal has no reason to be jealous of your ass and what happened earlier had nothing to do with Royal chasing him, because he was the one chasing her," Emerie chimed in.

"Em shut up, this has nothing to do with you."

"I got this Emerie," I said, getting up and walking towards Bia.

"You say I'm jealous but can't give me a reason as to why I would be jealous of you. But I can give you several reason as to why you're jealous of me," I told her, standing my grown. I was tired of this bitch thinking she could say whatever she wanted to me.

"Please tell me why I would be jealous of a little ass girl?" Bia said, laughing.

"First of all, I graduated high school. Have you? Second, I got my own shit. I'm the independent woman you want to be but because you don't know how to be on your own, you depend on niggas for any and everything you want. Third and lastly, I'ma 17-year-old child that took your man with little to no effort," I told her.

Everyone in the shop was quiet as they waited to see what was going to happen next. I honestly was over this whole dumb ass situation. Bia was quiet and didn't look like she was going to say anything. I turned around and started walking back to my desk when Bia grabbed me by my shirt, dragging me to the floor.

As soon as I hit the floor she started throwing punches. I'm not gonna lie, she had the upper hand on me until Emerie and Justice jumped in. Once I was able to get up, I pulled my hair into a quick bun and started pulling Emerie and Justice off her.

"Y'all chill, I got this!" I said once I got them away from her.

"Nah fuck that Royal, she did some bitch shit just now," Justice said, fuming from the mouth.

"Bia what you did was some pussy shit but it's not all your fault because I turned my back on the enemy which was a dumb move. But right now you're going to get your ass up and we are going to go outside and shoot the fair one," I said, pissed the hell off.

I walked away from her and took my ass outside. I was glad as hell I didn't have Paige with me today. Right after I walked outside the whole shop came out, with Bia being the head of the pack. I threw my hands up and she did the same. I let her throw the first couple of punches because I wasn't worried about her. The last one she threw connected and I was pissed that she hit me in my face. I started throwing punches left and right, landing every one. Bia started backing up from me and ended up slipping on gravel and falling right on her ass. I stood over her and delivering blow after blow until someone picked me up in the air.

"Get the fuck off of me before I beat your ass next!" I yelled out, mad that someone saved Bia from this ass whoopin' I was giving her.

"You aren't gonna do shit Slim so shut the fuck up," the person said. I instantly recognized the voice as Pharaoh's.

He carried me into the shop, dropped me on the floor and stood in front of the shop doors so no one could get in and I couldn't get out.

"I come over here to bring your ass lunch and I see you fighting out in the streets like you some bird bitch," he lectured, biting his bottom lip.

"I'm not a bird bitch and if you didn't come up in here earlier kissing me and shit this would have never happened!" I yelled at him.

"You fighting bitches over me?" he laughed.

"No, I'm fighting bitches because Bia thinks she can say and do whatever the fuck she wants and everything is just going to be okay."

"Fuck all that! All I know is I better not catch your ass fighting in these streets again!" He turned back towards the door opened it and told all the ladies to get their shit and leave because the shop was going to be closed for the rest of the day

Everyone walked in avoiding eye contact with me. Justice and Emerie got their stuff and stood next to me. The last one out the shop was Bia and she looked like she had something to say, but the look on Pharaoh's face told her she better keep walking.

"So what we about to do?" Justice asked.

"Royal bout to take her ass home," Pharaoh answered for me.

I looked at him as if he was crazy. My own mama didn't even tell me what to do.

"Don't listen to him, I'm about to go back to the crib and change and then we can do whatever."

"I'll catch up with y'all later, I'm about to go home and take a nap. I had too much drama for one day," Emerie sighed, walking out the door.

"You need a ride? Because Royal won't be coming back out," Pharaoh said to Justice as he locked up the shop's doors.

"Nah I'm straight, I drove. By the way, I'm Justice," she introduced herself. I forgot that they never really met.

"Wassup, I'm Pharaoh. Royal you ready to go?" he asked, looking down at me.

"I guess I have to go home now," I said laughing.

"You better go 'head before he beat that ass," she joked.

"He ain't beating shit, but I'll hit you up later," I chuckled, giving her a hug.

We both got in the car and Pharaoh drove off. I thought we were going to Pharaoh's house but we ended up going to the apartment I was moving into.

"What are we doing here?" I asked, getting out the car.

"Just come on," he said, taking my hand and leading me to the door.

He unlocked the door and flicked on the light. The living room was fully furnished with all black leather furniture. I walked towards the back of the house to look at the bedrooms and they too were fully furnished. I was in awe at everything and beyond grateful for everything Pharaoh had done for me so far.

"Oh my gosh! Pharaoh, when did you do all of this?" I asked, jumping on him and giving him a hug.

"Get down Slim, I got something else you can climb up on," he said, carrying me over to the couch and sitting me down on his lap.

"Shut up, but for real when did you do this?" I asked again.

"When you told me you were going to take the place I had my mom order some stuff for you."

"Thank you and I'll be sure to tell your mother thank you!" I said, looking around smiling.

"You don't have to thank me Slim, just do right by me," he said, looking me in the eyes.

At that moment, I knew Pharaoh was who I wanted to be with. I wasn't in love with him yet, but my feelings for him were starting to run deep.

"As long as you do right by me you don't ever have to worry about me doing you wrong," I told him and leaned forward for a kiss. Our tongues danced around each other before hands started to roam.

His hands explored my body and my hands did the same. I was long overdue for some action but I didn't want to rush into it either. I pulled away from the kiss and started to giggle.

"What are you laughing at Slim?"

"Nothing, I just haven't felt like this in a while and I don't want to rush it."

"Royal, we don't have to do anything you don't want to do."

"Do you always say the right things?" I asked him.

"Nah, I just say whatever is on my mind, it's that simple Slim."

"Yea whatever, let me go jump in the shower and change clothes so I can go pick up Paige," I said, standing up.

"My mom said she's gonna keep Paige overnight so don't even worry about it, but you do need to go and jump in the shower though," he laughed.

"Kiss my ass Pharaoh!" I laughed and went in the back to jump in the shower. I went into my room first to look in my drawers for some underclothes, when I realized I didn't have any of my clothes.

"Pharaoh, can you go to your house and bring back my stuff and Paige's too?" I yelled out so he could hear me.

"I got you. There are towels, wash cloths and body wash in the linen closet," he yelled back.

I smiled as I went to the linen closet and grabbed everything I needed. Pharaoh was so thoughtful, hopefully he stayed this way and didn't change.

I got out the shower and lotioned up with the Victoria Secret lotion that was in the cabinet. Once I was done, I walked to the front of the apartment to see if Pharaoh had made his way back yet. The house was empty and I didn't want to walk around ass naked so I kept the towel wrapped around me and laid on the bed.

"Wake that ass up!" Pharaoh shouted, slapping me on the ass.

I rolled over annoyed, because if it was one thing that I hated, it was to be woken up out of my sleep.

"What took you so long?" I asked him, sitting up in the bed trying to get some of the sleep out of my eyes.

"I stopped and got some food because I didn't think you would want to cook."

"Oh thanks." I got up to look through the bags of stuff so I could put on some clothes when Pharaoh grabbed me. He started kissing me. He started with my lips and then travelled down to my nipples. From nibbling to biting and then to sucking, he kept switching up making my knees shake. I let my hand travel down to his tool and didn't know if I was ready for what I was feeling. From the feel of it, Pharaoh was working with a monster; it was both long and thick.

"You like that don't you?" he whispered in my ear.

"Mhmmmmm," I moaned.

"Let me take you," he groaned, lifting me up, causing my towel to fall and then laying me on the bed. I watched as he stripped out of his clothes in amazement. God broke the mold when He created Pharaoh because his body was perfect. He got on the bed and placed the head at my opening, playing in my wetness.

"You ready Royal, because once we go here there is no going back. You mine's for life after this," he stated, looking deep into my eyes with his grey ones.

"I'm ready," I moaned.

He eased his way into me and started stroking slow, hitting spots I didn't even know were there. I had only been with one other nigga and he didn't make me feel half the things I was feeling with Pharaoh. If this is what cloud 9 felt like then I wanted to be up there forever. That night I gave myself to Pharaoh in more ways than one, and he gave his self to me.

Chapter 6

"Girl it's about time we got together and went out. Between work, Paige and Pharaoh I never get any time with you." Justice complained.

"You know if you wanted to chill with me all you had to do was send a text, don't act like that," I told her, fingering my hair in the mirror.

"You say that now but when the time comes you're gonna be like, 'I can't, I'm with Pharaoh,'" she said laughing.

"I'm not even with him the majority of the time."

"Yea right, y'all are glued at the hip but it's cute though, I'm happy for you mama."

"Now let's go before I change my mind, you know I don't do clubs," I said, leading the way out of the house.

"Did you even tell Pharaoh you were going?" she asked once we got in the car.

"I didn't tell him exactly where I was going, but I told him I was going out."

"Oh well, doesn't matter to me as long as we turn up!" she said, turning up the music.

I just laughed at her because she was truly a party animal. We were on our way to this club called Liquid, it was supposed to be the hot spot. I pulled into the parking lot and it was jammed packed. I found a place to park over to the far left of the club. We got out and saw that the line was wrapped around the building. I looked at Justice letting her know that I wasn't about to stand in this long ass line.

"Don't even trip," she said, walking towards the front of the line.

"I know these two stuck up bitches are not gonna act like they don't see this line," Some chick yelled.

I looked out to see who it was, and it was Bia's raggedy ass.

"Bia shut the fuck up before I beat that ass again," I told her and strutted my way in the club. I knew some shit was going to pop off if they let Bia into the club.

"Don't even worry about her, let's go have some fun," Justice said, pulling me over to the bar. We ordered two shots of henny and threw them back as fast as we ordered them. I wasn't a heavy drinker so that little shot of henny had me going.

"Let's go dance," Justice said, taking my hand and leading me to the dance floor.

I started dancing and moving my hips to the beat when someone grabbed me close and pulled me towards him. The DJ was playing, Song's on 12 Play, by Chris Brown and Trey Songz and I was lost in the song. Dude and I were moving in sync. To others it looked like we were lovers, but I didn't know this fool from a hole in the wall.

"You dance like this with everybody?" the stranger asked.

"Not really, but I like this song and you seem to know what you're doing," I told him.

"Royal, I always know what I'm doing," The stranger said.

When he said my name, I pulled away from him to see who he was and how he knew my name.

Looking up I saw that it was Pharaoh. He was dressed in all black and his eyes were sitting real low. Just the sight of him had me ready to run off in the corner, and right on cue the DJ started playing, Love in this Club remix.

"Slim what you doing in the club dressed like you don't got a man?"

"I look cute! There is nothing wrong with what I have on," I said, doing a little spin for him. I was rocking a leather short jumpsuit with fish net stockings and black ankle boots.

"Let's go up to my office and chill," Pharaoh said, taking my hand.

"What do you mean your office?"

"I mean exactly what I said."

"Hold up let me go find Justice and tell her where I'm going."

"Ight, just meet me by the bar."

I gave him a kiss and went to go find Justice. I didn't know where she had gone off too. I circled the club at least twice and couldn't find her. I sent her a text telling her to call me so I knew that she was cool. I started making my way to the bar , but when I got close enough I saw Bia all up in Pharaoh's face. For a minute I stood there and watched how it was going to play out, this would be the moment of truth.

Bia kept caressing his leg and every time she did Pharaoh would push her hand off him. I felt like I watched enough and that my presence was needed to calm the situation down.

"Bae you ready to go?" I asked, walking in between the both of them.

"I know this bitch didn't! I'm so tired of your prissy ass walking around like you run shit, when you know damn well that the only thing you run is up that pole over at Chix & Dix," Bia slurred.

I didn't know how she knew, but I wasn't going to let her know that the shit she just said got to me.

"You're right. I ran up that pole, slid down it and ended up on the dick that you so desperately want," I turned around and told her.

"Fuck you and that nigga, don't nobody want his ass."

"Yea whatever," I muttered and turned my back to her to grab Pharaoh's hand so we could leave. I didn't take two steps before I was being pulled down by my hair. Pharaoh must have grabbed her off me because once I hit the floor I jumped up ready to fuck something up.

"Bia you out of line. I'ma give you a pass because you drunk but if you ever put your hands on Royal again I will fucking leave your body in a ditch," Pharaoh warned, pushing her towards the bar.

"You gonna pick a fucking 17-year-old stripper over me nigga?!!" she yelled.

"Just a minute ago you didn't want me, remember?" he said, laughing.

"I'ma give your ass something to laugh at," she slurred, grabbing a bottle off the bar counter and throwing it at Pharaoh. Bia had to be drunk because the bottle didn't even make it him.

"Royal let's go," Pharaoh said, walking off.

Before I followed him, I had to teach Bia a lesson. She was still standing at the bar with her back facing me.

"Bia," I called after her.

"The fuck do you….." I cut her sentence short with a punch to her face. I watched her hold her face as she struggled to get up. I left her ass right there and went over to where Pharaoh was. We got on the elevator without speaking to each other. If Bia was going to be a constant issue in our relationship then I wasn't going to put up with the bullshit.

We got off and went into the office that I didn't even know he had. I took a seat and started rubbing my temples because my head was throbbing.

"Here take this," Pharaoh offered, passing me a couple of pills and a bottle of water. I popped the pills in my mouth and drunk the water.

"Slim you 'ight"?

"I'm fine," I said with an attitude. I know I shouldn't be mad at him but I couldn't help it because he was part of the reason Bia acted the way she did.

"Wassup Royal, why you talking to me like I did something to you?"

"Nothing."

"Royal stop it, if something is bothering you then speak on it," he said, leaning back in his chair.

"What's bothering me is that I'm not about to be a part of this love triangle."

"What are you even talking about? Who is in a love triangle?" he asked with a look of confusion.

"Look, if Bia is going to continue to be a problem then I can't do this."

"Slim you getting mad over stuff I can't control. She came over to the bar and was rubbing on a nigga and I was moving her hands away and telling her to chill. What more did you want me to do?"

"You shouldn't have fucked with her in the first place!" I yelled.

"I'm not even going to respond to that dumb shit you just said."

"Why is it dumb because it's the truth? You called yourself trying to get with me but you had her riding shot gun."

"You were the one that wanted to play hard to get, so I found someone to occupy my time until you stopped playing games."

"First of all I wasn't playing hard to get because I *am* hard to get. Second, I really wasn't trying to fuck with you but your ass just kept coming."

"Slim don't play with me. You're saying you with me because a nigga wore you down?"

"Basically," I said, shrugging my shoulders.

"Ight you ready to go?" he asked, getting up.

"Uh, I'm waiting for Justice to call me, hold on here she go now," I said, pulling out my phone.

"Royal where are you?" Justice asked.

"I'm upstairs in Pharaoh's office."

"Office? Why does he have an office?"

"He says he owns the club, but I'm about to leave," I told her.

"Okay, do you have a ride or you want me to drive you?"

"Pharaoh is going to drive me home," I told her.

"Okay cool, 'cause I'm chilling with some dude I met."

"Ight Justice, be careful and text me when you get home."

"I got you, don't worry," she said and hung up the phone.

"Yea we can go, Justice is saying," I told Pharaoh.

Pharaoh said a couple things to a few people before we headed out the back of the club. The entire car ride was silent. I knew that I had no right to have an attitude with him but I was pissed off about the whole situation. I didn't like being disrespected, and Bia came with disrespect every time I saw her.

"You gonna get out?" Pharaoh asked, pulling me out of my thoughts. I was so caught up in my thoughts I didn't even notice we were at my house.

"Are you coming in?" I asked him, hoping he would say yes.

"Nah, I'm gonna crash at the crib."

"Pharaoh, why are you acting like that?"

"Remember ma, you didn't really want me, you just with a nigga because I kept coming around."

"I didn't mean for it to come out like that," I said.

"Yea 'ight Slim, but on the real I can find a chick who wants to be with a nigga simply for me being me. I don't need a chick that's only gonna fuck with me because I wore her down."

"Can you get out the car please?" I pouted. I knew I fucked up and I had to fix it fast because the truth was that I liked Pharaoh, I liked him a lot. I just wasn't sure if this shit was going to work.

"What you want Slim? I'm trying to leave," Pharaoh said, getting out the car.

I stood in front of him and gazed into his grey eyes before I started talking. I want to make sure that what I felt was right or if I was caught up in him playing captain save-a-hoe.

"I know what I said earlier was hurtful and I'm sorry for that, but it was the truth. I wasn't trying to fuck with you because I had other things I needed to focus on, but the reason I gave in is because I liked you. No matter how much I tried to push your ass away you just kept coming back which made me like you more," I told him truthfully.

"I hear you Royal, but I'm still about to go crash. I'll pick lil sis up from my mom's tomorrow and bring her over here in the morning," he said, kissing me on the cheek.

I watched him as he got in his car and pulled the away. Even after I couldn't see his car anymore, I stood there wondering if I just fucked up a good thing or not.

Chapter 7

I couldn't sleep at all last night, which is why I'm up early in the morning now. It was a Saturday and Pharaoh was supposed to bring Paige home from his mother's house. I got myself out of bed and decided to cook breakfast for the three of us. I knew Pharaoh was still mad from last night but I was hoping this breakfast would at least cheer him up a little bit. I went in the bathroom, brushed my teeth and washed my face. I couldn't have morning breath talking to a nigga like Pharaoh. I grabbed my phone before walking into the kitchen. I had a missed call from Pharaoh and a text from him saying he was on his way. I smiled, put my phone down and started cooking. Thirty minutes later breakfast was done; I made cheese eggs, bacon, sausage, pancakes and grits. There was no way Pharaoh was going to see all of this food and still have an attitude with me.

An hour passed before I heard a knock at my door. I looked at myself in the mirror in the hallway that led to the door. I swung the door hoping to see Paige with Pharaoh but it was Paige and his mother.

"Royal I missed you!" Paige said, running in and giving me a hug.

"I missed you too, that's why you rolling with me today."

"Yes!! Where are we going?" she asked, as I closed the door and led the way to the kitchen.

"It's a surprise, now go put your stuff up in the room and then come back down here so you can eat," I told her.

"Okay!" she said and ran into her room.

"You didn't look to happy to see me," Ms. King said, sitting out the table.

"I'm always happy to see you Ms. King," I told her pulling down three plates from the cabinet.

"You don't have to call me Ms. King. I told you before that you can call me Adira."

"You want a plate Adira?" I asked, laughing because I wasn't comfortable calling her that just yet.

"You know I do but I also want to talk to you about my son."

Before I could respond, Paige came back into the kitchen and sat next to Adira.

"Paige you ready to eat?"

"Yea," she said.

I made her and Adira a plate and brought it to them before I went back and made my own plate. The entire time I was eating, I was wondering why she wanted to talk to me about Pharaoh. I mean yeah we were dating, but it wasn't anything too serious, at least I thought it wasn't anything too serious. Paige was the first one done eating. She washed her plate and went into her room to watch TV.

"I didn't wanna have this conversation in front of Paige but now that she's in her room let's talk."

"Okay," I said looking down, playing with my food. I was too caught up in my thoughts to even think about food right now.

"What are your intensions with my son?"

"Uh I don't know, we just started this relationship," I answered. The question caught me off guard and I didn't know what to say.

"You don't have to feel uncomfortable Royal, I'm only asking because I know my son and I know every mother says that, but I really know my son. I have never seen him talk about a chick as much as he talks about you."

"No disrespect Adira, but anyone can talk. For me it's all about the actions."

"His actions don't match up because if you ask me they go hand in hand."

"I'm not trying to put his business out there," I said, not really wanting to talk about this.

"Chile please, I'm his mother not some chick on the street."

"Okay. I'm just not sure that he and Bia are fucking around still. I mean, when he was supposed to be all into me he had Bia riding shot gun. Now I'm not mad at that because we weren't together, but then I'm out in the club and Bia is all in his face in the bar."

"First off let me say that if he did have Bia riding shot gun it was probably only to make you jealous because he told me about how you kept telling him you just wanted to be friends. Now don't get me wrong, him trying to make you jealous is a bitch move but I can see that it worked," she laughed.

I just looked at her because I didn't want to get disrespectful, but I didn't find anything funny.

"Royal fix your face, I'm just joking. Now as far as the thing at the bar, was he entertaining Bia?"

"No, he was pushing her off of him."

"Okay then, so what's the problem?"

"My problem is that I don't want Bia to be a constant issue in our relationship."

"Royal, you never let another chick push you away from your dude, especially when he's not doing you wrong."

"I'm not letting her push me away."

"Royal yes you are. I mean if it's that easy for you to just up and leave then you don't deserve my son."

"Why don't I deserve your son?" I asked, raising my voice a little. I was starting to get defensive because she was his mother not mine, so how could she tell who I wanted.

"My son deserves someone that is going to be there for him. He hasn't done anything wrong but you're ready to call it quits because of what the next chick did. All I'm saying is really think about it before you let a good one go," she advised and got up.

I assumed she went to go say bye to Paige because she walked towards the back room. I started clearing off the table when she came back to the front and told me she would see me Monday at work. I nodded my head and waved bye. I was upset a little because everything she said was right, I just didn't want to hear it. I knew Pharaoh was a good dude but Bia was gonna get hurt fucking with me. I already had to fight her twice and I didn't wanna go at it with her a third time. If I wanted to continue this relationship with Pharaoh, I had to show Bia that I don't play when it comes to my shit. Those two ass beatings didn't do it but I knew something that would.

******

I was nervous as hell as I walked into the Brooklyn College Admission building. I only had about two more weeks to apply before the deadline and I wanted to get all the information I needed to make sure this was a good fit.

"Royal why are we here?" Paige asked, looking around.

"I'm signing up for school."

"Are you going to go to the same school as me?"

"No I'm going to a grown up school."

"Can I go to a grown up school too?"

"When you get older you can, now go have a seat while I talk to this lady," I told her. I watched her go over to the seating area before I gave the receptionist my attention.

"Hi... Umm, I was wondering if there was someone I could talk to about applying here?"

"You know the deadline is in two weeks right?" the lady said. I looked at her as if to say, 'did I ask you that'?

"Yes I know that, which is why I asked you if I could talk to someone."

"What's your name?"

"Royal."

"Okay Royal," she said, looking me up and down. "Go have a seat and someone will be with you."

I rolled my eyes at her and took a seat next to Paige. If the admissions lady was as rude as her receptionist was then we were going to have a problem.

"Royal I miss mom," Paige said, playing with her necklace.

"I'm sure she misses you too."

"Can we go see her?"

"Sure, once we leave here we can go."

"Yess!!!" she said excitedly.

"Here, take my phone and practice spelling today's words."

She took my phone and went straight to the spelling bee app. I had to keep her busy because I didn't want her asking any more questions about Aria, especially ones I didn't have the answers to. I hadn't talked to or seen my mother since the day she was throwing my shit out of her house. If it was up to me I would never let Aria see Paige again, but I couldn't keep Paige away from her. Paige didn't understand what was going on and I didn't feel like at her age she needed to know what was going on.

"Royal?" An older white lady called out.

"I'm here," I said, standing up and grabbing Paige's hand.

"Follow me please."

I followed her into the next room. It was cute little office but it needed more space. I took a seat and placed Paige on my lap.

"Okay, first off let me start by saying thank you for expressing your interest in Brooklyn College. My name is Layla. How can I help you?"

"I just wanted to talk to you a little about the school before I applied."

"Okay, well as you know the deadline for the application is in two weeks, but I can help you get on the right path with that. What are you looking to major in and what kind of degree do you want?"

For about an hour, we went back and forth asking and answering each other's questions. Once it was over, I had applied and only had to do my fasfa. Layla told me it would take about a month for me to find out if I was accepted or not. I walked out of there feeling good about myself. Hopefully going to see my mother wouldn't mess that up.

We got on the Q- train and took that half an hour ride. When we came from underground, I looked down at my phone and realized that Pharaoh hadn't sent me a text or anything all day. I wanted to send him a text but after the conversation I had with his mom earlier I figured I would wait.

I grabbed Paige's hand because our stop was the stop coming up. We got off and walked the short walk to our mother's house. Walking up to the door, I felt a little uneasy like something was wrong. I pushed the feeling to the side and knocked four times before someone came to the door.

"Who you?" an older guy with salt and pepper hair asked. Just from looking at him, I could tell he hadn't taken a shower in days. Not to mention the awful body odor that was coming off him.

"Umm where is Aria?" I asked, trying not to inhale his scent.

"She's not here."

"Do you know where she is?"

"Nope, she hasn't been here in over a month."

"Well if you see her tell her that Royal is looking for her."

"Ight lil mama."

I grabbed Paige and walked away from the door. I didn't know who that nigga was, but I hope my mother was okay wherever she was.

"Where's mom?" Paige asked, as we walked up the street.

"I don't know but don't worry, I'll find her. What do you wanna do now?"

"I wanna go see Macy."

"Ight let's go," I said.

I waved down a dollar cab, hopped in, gave the cabbie the address and sent Justice a text letting her know that Paige and I were on our way over. The whole ride all I could think about was my mother. My mother and I didn't get along but I still loved her and didn't want anything to happen. I wasn't that big in praying but I did say a quick prayer to keep my mother safe and well.

Chapter 8

"Royal what are you doing here?" Justice asked, opening the door for Paige and me.

"Paige wanted to see Macy, and I sent your ass a text saying we were on our way."

"Paige you can go upstairs, Macy is in her room," Justice told Paige. I waited until Paige was out of earshot before going in on her. I hadn't spoken to her since last night at the club and from the looks of it, she was just now waking up. Her hair was all over the place and her too short robe was showing more than it was supposed to, so I knew that she brought someone home with her.

"You're just now waking up? You must have had a good night after I left," I teased, going in her fridge and getting something to drink.

"Get out of my fridge and let's go upstairs so I can put you on," she said, grabbing a container of ice cream out the freezer.

"Girl stop looking around my room no one is in here," she laughed.

I laughed too because I was looking for someone to jump out of the closet or something. I sat on her dresser because she had clothes thrown all over her bed.

"You need to clean this room, it's a mess!" I lectured.

"Shut up, I had plans on cleaning it today, but what happened with you and Pharaoh last night? I didn't know he owned that club,"

Justice said, putting a spoon full of ice cream in her mouth. I didn't know if I should tell her what happened between Pharaoh and me because I didn't want her throwing shade.

"I didn't either, but we didn't stay long at the club," I told her, not giving much detail.

"I seen Bia last night," she said, smirking at me.

"What are you telling me for, I don't care about her."

"I know you don't, which is why you beat her ass."

"What are you talking about?"

"Don't play dumb, I saw Bia pull you down but before I could do anything Pharaoh pulled her off you. I figured y'all had it handled so I left."

"Oh really, and who did you leave with?" I asked.

"Nah don't try and change the subject, what happened?"

"Nothing happened. I left Pharaoh at the bar so I could go find you and when I came back Bia was in his face. We had some words and when I went to leave, she pulled me down by my hair. Pharaoh said something to her and we left, but before we left I punched her in her face."

"You are crazy you know that?" Justice said, laughing out of control.

"I'm not crazy, Bia keeps trying me!"

"Shit I would have thought she would've learned her lesson with that first beat down you gave her."

"That's the same shit I said. But anyway, then me and Pharaoh got into it and when his mom dropped Paige off this morning she started telling me about how Pharaoh deserves someone that is going to ride for him and all this other bullshit," I said, rolling my eyes.

"I mean, I don't know too much about y'all relationship but he seems like he's good for you, plus he was all up your ass every time you would push him away."

"I don't wanna talk about this anymore. Who did you go home with last night?"

"Remember Raylon and Zalen from school? They were juniors when we were freshmen?"

"Yea what about them?"

"Well I ran into the both of them last night and girl they are still fine as hell."

"Tell me you didn't do what I think you did?"

"Bitch no I didn't, I might do some freaky things but I'm not that freaky. Anyway, me and Raylon were talking and one thing led to another and that is who I went home with."

"You always said you were gonna get him," I laughed. I use to have the biggest crush on Zalen. He was 6'4 with chocolate skin as smooth as a baby's bottom.

"Yea and he's mad cool and the sex was the bomb," she giggled.

"I bet, we use to have the biggest crushes on them."

"I know girl, hold up a second," she said, picking up her ringing cell phone.

I didn't want to be all in her business so I went to go check on Paige. When I walked into the other room, the girls were on the bed watching Sponge Bob.

"Royal are we leaving?" Paige asked, taking her eyes off the TV.

"No, but we will be leaving soon."

"I want to stay over and play with Macy."

"You don't want to leave with me?" I said, acting like I was hurt.

"I'll come with you tomorrow I promise," she begged.

"Okay, if Justice says it's okay you can stay."

"Yayyy!" Both girls yelled.

I left out the room shaking my head. Justice was still on the phone and it sounded like she was making plans for someone to come over.

"That was Raylon, he's about to come over and I told him to bring Zalen."

"Why would you tell him to bring Zalen? I'm not staying long, I was about to leave. Paige wanted to spend the night but I'ma take her home since you have company."

"At least meet Zalen before you leave and can you take Macy with you because I'm going to be a little busy tonight."

"Yea I'll take her," I said, rolling my eyes at her. Justice was my girl and all but sometimes, I thought she was too caught up in dick.

"Let me go make myself presentable because I look a mess. Let the boys in for me when they get here please," she said, going off into the bathroom.

I shook my head at her while I dialed the number for a cab service; there was no way I was taking both Macy and Paige on the train with me.

"Yes I need a cab to 13th Avenue in Williamsburg," I said as soon as the guy came on the phone.

"Okay, where are you being picked up from?"

"180 Montague Street in Brooklyn."

"Okay cab will be there in 30 minutes."

"Wait, how much is it?"

"It's going to be $50."

"50 dollars? You bugging!" I said and hung up the phone. There was no way I was going to pay $50 dollars for a cab.

I decided to call the only person I knew that would come and pick me up.

"Wassup Slim?" Pharaoh asked, answering the phone on the third ring.

"Nothing, at Justice's house. I was wondering if you could come pick me up because I have both Paige and Macy and I don't wanna take them on the train."

"You don't have to explain, I got you. Just text me the address and I'll be there soon."

"Thank you so much," I said and hung up the phone.

I got off the phone and heard someone knocking at the door. I sent Pharaoh the address and threw my phone on the bed. I stopped at the mirror that was before the front door to make sure I looked okay. I wasn't sure why I did it, but I felt the need to be on point. Once I was satisfied with my looks, I opened the front door and was met by my high school crush.

"Uh come on in, y'all can have a seat in the living room," I offered, moving out the way so they could come in the door. I closed the door behind me and sat across from the two feeling uncomfortable. I didn't wanna be there, but Justice was still upstairs getting dressed and I couldn't leave them alone.

"Your name is Royal right?" Zalen asked, leaning forward.

"Yea."

"You grew up ma," Raylon said, eyeing me and licking his lips.

Raylon was the player out of the two, which was why I never liked his ass. Don't get me wrong, he was cute but he was known to fuck with best friends and then have them fight over him and I wasn't about to go through that.

"Yea I did, but let me go check on Justice real quick," I said and damn near ran up the stairs. I went into Macy's room first and told the girls to get their things and to come downstairs when they were ready to go. I then went into Justice's room to see if she had pulled herself together and to my surprise she did. Her hair was done and the clothes that were once spread all over her room were gone.

"Your boy is down stairs," I told her, grabbing my phone and bag.

"Okay, send him up and send me a text when you leave," she said, giving me a hug.

"Just be careful please," I told her.

"I'm always careful you know this."

I nodded my head at her and went back downstairs. They guys were sitting there like this was the last place they wanted to be.

"Raylon, Justice said you can go upstairs."

"Ight, Za you don't have to wait here for a nigga. Since I rode with you I'll just call a cab when I'm ready to be out," he said and went upstairs leaving Zalen and me alone.

There was this awkward silence between us. I was wishing like hell that Pharaoh would hurry the hell up.

"Royal how you been?" Zalen asked, breaking the silence.

"I'm good, I just graduated high school and I plan on starting college in the fall."

"You graduated already? I thought you were two years behind me?"

"I was, but I had the chance to take some extra classes and graduate early."

"Smart and beautiful, they don't make them like you anymore." The way he was looking at me had me feeling the same things I felt when Pharaoh looked at me, which wasn't a good thing.

"I'm not special, trust me."

"Yea right, but wassup with you? When can I take you out? Justice told me how much you was feeling me back in high school." When he said that I wanted to run upstairs and slap the shit out of Justice.

"I wouldn't say I was feeling you, I just thought you were cute and as far as you taking me out on a date, I really don't have time for dating right now."

Before he could say anything back, I got text from Pharaoh saying he was outside. I called upstairs for Macy and Paige to come down.

"I'm sorry to cut our conversation short but my ride is outside."

"If you needed a ride I could have took you where you needed to go."

"Don't worry about it. Paige, take Macy to Pharaoh's car," I told the girls once they came downstairs.

"Who's Pharaoh? Your nigga?" Zalen asked, picking up the bags Paige and Macy left on the floor.

"Something like that," I said, holding the door for him.

Pharaoh was watching me like a hawk when Zalen and I walked towards his car. I took the bags from Zalen and put them in trunk.

"Thank you for the carrying the bags," I told him, closing the trunk.

"No problem ma, if you ever need help with anything else get at me," Zalen said, walking off in the direction of an all black Mercedes Benz. I hurried around to the front to get in the passenger seat.

"Who was that?" Pharaoh asked as soon as I got in.

"No one, he's just a friend from school. There's nothing for you to worry about daddy, you know I'm yours," I said, leaning over and giving him a kiss. Not talking to Pharaoh all day had me missing him like crazy.

"That's your word?"

"Yea that's my word. Your mom talked to me this morning and helped me realize a couple of things. Pharaoh I like you and I want to see where we can go with this, but if we are going to do this then I need honesty from you. I want to know what you do for a living and anything else that I need to know, and in return for your honesty I'm going to give you my loyalty and my heart."

"You sure you ready for this shit Royal?"

"I'm sure, I promise you."

"Ight, when we get in the house I'll tell you everything."

I nodded my head and enjoyed the rest of the ride to the house. I felt like Pharaoh knew everything about me and I didn't know anything about him, which is why I was so hesitant about being with him. After this talk, I hoped everything would be good between us.

******

"The girls are in bed, now let's talk," I said, getting on the bed sitting Indian style across from Pharaoh.

"Ight this is how this is going to go, we going question for question."

"Okay, I'll go first. How do you make your money?" This was one of the most important questions I could ask. I don't think I could deal with a nigga hugging the block and coming in all times of the night. Now that I think about it, Pharaoh always came by my house no later than ten, so he couldn't be a corner boy.

"I set up buyers with sellers."

"That's it?"

"That's all you need to know Slim. I'm sure I don't have to sit and spell out exactly what I'm setting up the sellers to buy."

"I guess," I said, shrugging it off.

"Where's your pops?" he asked.

"I don't know and I really don't care. My father has never been in my life and I'm okay with that," I answered honestly. When I was younger, I used to wonder who he was and why he didn't want me. After watching my mom though, I started to understand more and never really cared after that.

"You never wanted to find him or anything?" Pharaoh asked.

"Nah. How long have you owned the club?" I asked.

"Since I was 20. I opened that club and the salon at the same time. It was a way for me to clean up my money. What happened with your first love?"

"How do you know I was ever in love?" I asked.

"I can from the way you act. You try to act as if you don't have time for a relationship because of Paige, but really it's because someone hurt you and you don't wanna go through that again. Instead of letting a nigga in, you focus all your time on Paige," he observed, reading me like a book.

"You're right, but looking back at the relationship I wasn't in love, it was more of a crush. I thought what we had was love but once I gave him what he wanted he just stopped talking to me all together," I admitted, shaking my head. Having to go through that alone really fucked with me because I didn't know how to handle it.

"That's fucked up Slim, but you can't let what one nigga did fuck it up for every other nigga, especially 'cause that shit happened while you were in high school. A lot of high school relationships can't be taken seriously."

"Yea I know but I'm trying, which is why I'm sitting here with your big headed ass," I laughed, punching him in his arm.

"You one to talk about a big head, but I don't say much."

"Aye, don't talk about my head. Why did you start messing with Bia?"

"Man why you have to go and bring her up?" he said, sucking his teeth. I really didn't care how much he sucked his teeth, he was going to answer this question because this was something I needed to know.

"Come on, we said we were going to be honest with each other. Is it because she was more around your age range?"

"I never messed with Bia, all we did was talk. She was just making it more than what it really was."

"Uh huh, I'ma let that answer rock for now," I replied, not really knowing if I should believe him or not.

"Wassup with you and dude that came out the house?"

"I already told you he is someone I went to school with, nothing more nothing less."

"Yea 'ight Slim, I'ma let you keep saying that."

"Is Pharaoh jealous?"

"Nah, a nigga like me has no reason to be jealous because if I feel like there is more going on than what you say, that nigga is dead and you're gonna be alone," he answered, smirking.

"Oh really?" I said, straddling him.

"Yea, don't look surprised. There are three things I don't play with; my family, my girl and loyalty." The look in his eye let me know that he was serious.

"You don't have to worry about me playa."

"I better not have to. Now show daddy how you ride a horse," he said, smacking my ass.

Standing up on the bed, I pulled my shirt of over my head, unbuttoned my pants and threw them on the floor. I slipped my panties off, got back in the straddling position and shoved my panties in his mouth.

"Chill Slim, what are you doing?" he asked, taking my panties out his mouth and throwing them on the floor.

"Sssshhhhhh," I said, putting my finger up to his lips. I slithered down towards the end of the bed, unzipped his jeans and took off his boxers. I wrapped my hands around his dick, massaging it until it was at full attention.

I positioned myself over it so it would rub against my opening. I played into my wetness until Pharaoh pulled me down on his dick. I gasped for air because this was only my second time having sex with Pharaoh and I wasn't used to his size or thickness yet.

"You play too much Royal, give me what I want," he moaned, caressing my back.

I was moving my hips in a slow motion, making sure I felt all of him and he felt all of me. He reached up and started playing with my nipples. The way he was tugging on them had me ready to explode. I learned forward and put one of them in his month.

"Don't be gentle," I whispered in his ear.

"Slim you a freak," he groaned, biting down on my nipple.

I was so caught up in the whole thing I didn't even realize I was moaning loud enough for the neighbors to hear me.

"Mhmmmm Pharaoh, cum with me," I moaned.

I picked up the pace and within minutes, we both let loose. It felt like I had let out everything that was in my body. I slumped over on Pharaoh's chest and wasn't ready to move. All I wanted to do was sleep at that point.

"You wore your little ass out?" Pharaoh said, rubbing my back and laughing.

"Shut up, don't act like you didn't enjoy it."

"Of course I did, you got gold in between your legs Slim."

"Which is why I'm named Royal," I said, laughing my ass off at my own corny joke.

"That wasn't even funny Slim."

"Whatever."

"I love you Slim," he said, kissing me on the forehead.

"Are you sure you mean that? We just met each other and I don't know much about love, but I think it takes more than two months to fall in love," I said, keeping it a buck.

"Everyone is different, I'm not one of those 'suckas for love' but I know how I feel. I see potential in you ma. I see your fight and determination to make it in this world for you and your sister. Everything that I see in you Slim is the reason why I love you. So yea, I'm sure I love you and that I'm in love with you."

"I don't know what to say."

"You don't have to say anything. Just because I said it doesn't mean you have to say it. I just wanted to let you know how I felt, and I know that when you're ready you will let me know how you feel."

After he said that I was on the verge of tears, everything he just said made me respect him even more. My feelings for Pharaoh ran deep, but I don't think I was at the point to say I was in love.

"Are you crying Royal? Don't get all soft on me now," Pharaoh said, wiping my tears.

"Shut up, you're the one that was just being soft."

"Nah Slim, don't get it twisted. I was being real, not soft."

"I respect it," I said, laughing.

"Ight cool, now go get the remote."

I got up, grabbed the remote for him, came back and cuddled in his chest. I was feeling on top of the world right now. I had a dude that loved me and wasn't pressuring me to feel the same. I stopped stripping and had a job that was taking care of my sister and me. I had my own crib and I was starting school in the fall. Everything seemed to be falling into place and I was more than happy about it all.

Chapter 9

The weekend went by way too fast for me. Saturday night was amazing and on Sunday I just spent time in the house until it was time for me to bring Macy home. Justice wasn't there but her mother was so I left Macy with her. I needed to have a talk with Justice because I didn't like how she didn't look out for Macy. I knew it was none of my business but I still felt Justice could do better.

I got in the shower to help clear my head of the thoughts of this weekend. It was time to get back to work. I hoped Bia's dumb ass wasn't there because I didn't wanna deal with any drama. After getting out the shower, I threw on cut up denim shorts with a black wife beater and some Chanel sandals. I sprayed some perfume on, took out my rollers that were in my hair and was ready to get this day started.

"Paige, come so we can go," I said, walking into the kitchen and giving Pharaoh a kiss on the cheek.

"You need to get a car, I'm tired of driving your ass around," he said, slapping me on the ass.

"You love driving me around which is why you haven't brought me a car yet."

"I didn't buy you one because I didn't even know you could drive."

"I can drive but I rather you drive me places, that way I can keep an eye on you."

"Pharaoh!!" Paige yelled, running over to him. The relationship those two were forming was beautiful, especially because she didn't have a father figure in her life.

"Wassup baby sis, you acting like you haven't seen me in days," he said, smiling at her.

"I haven't seen you in days silly!" she laughed.

"You just saw me yesterday and the day before."

"Noooooo."

"Yes you did, but forget all of that, you ready to go?"

She nodded her head yes and ran out the door. I ran behind her because we were still new to this area and I didn't want anything to happen to her.

"Paige don't you ever run out of the house like that," I yelled.

"I'm sorry Royal, I was just trying to get the front seat before you," Paige pouted.

"Slim don't yell at her. She good, nothing gonna happen to her," Pharoah butted in.

"You don't know that Pharaoh."

"Chill your worrisome ass down and get in the car."

I buckled Paige in and got in the passenger seat. I didn't like Pharaoh telling me that I was wrong for yelling at my sister, but I let it slide because the start to my day was going good and I didn't want anything messing it up.

"Why are you so quiet over there?" Pharaoh asked, looking at me from the corner of his eye.

"No reason."

"Yea 'ight Royal. Look, I'm not coming back here tonight. I have some business I have to handle and I don't wanna come in your spot all late when I know baby sis is going to be there."

"It's cool I guess, just be safe."

"I'm always safe Slim, you don't ever have to worry."

"I bet you are," I told him.

In no time, we were in front of the shop. I got out and helped Paige out of the backseat. I walked her in the salon before going back out to say goodbye to Pharaoh.

"You coming in or nah?" I asked him, leaning in the driver's side window.

"Nah, I don't wanna start anything, you know y'all females be tripping."

"I don't trip, that be your other bitch. But I'ma catch you later," I said, kissing him.

"You're my only bitch," he said, driving off.

I laughed at him as I walked back into the salon. Walking towards the back I said hi to everyone I knew, I even spoke to Bia's ass. She rolled her eyes and I had to laugh because she was just so petty.

"Hey Royal, I was wondering if you was going to come back here and talk to me," Adira said.

"Of course I would come and talk to you, why wouldn't I?"

"I didn't think things ended well after that conversation we had."

"I felt some type of way during the conversation, but that was 2 days ago and I'm fine now. Plus, you only told me the truth and it was things I needed to hear."

"I wasn't trying to hurt you in anyway Royal. I look at both you and Paige as family."

"I know you do and I'm glad. I'm about to go answer some phones before anyone has anything to say. Paige I love you and be good back here."

"I love you too Royal," Paige said, never lifting her eyes from the laptop she was playing on.

I left out the back and went over to my desk because the phones were ringing off the hook and the girls in the shop acted as if they didn't know how to answer a phone. I was answering the phone back to back for at least thirty minutes before I got a break.

"I hope some of them calls were appointments for me," Emerie said, walking towards me. I hadn't seen this girl since I got into it with Bia.

"You know they were and where have you been miss? I haven't seen you in forever."

"I have been chilling, trying to get ready for my sophomore year of college."

"Speaking of college, I signed up the other day."

"Which school you wanna go to?"

"Brooklyn College. Hopefully I get in though."

"That's a good school and you know you're gonna get in, don't even second guess it. But let me get back to my station," she said, walking away.

I nodded my head at her and got back to work. I was only an hour into my shift and I was more than ready to go home.

******

There was an hour left before the shop closed. Everyone had already left except me, Emerie, Bia, and some other Spanish girl. Paige was still in the back on the laptop. I checked on her a few times and she was fine. I wish she had some friends to play with because she was always the only kid and I knew it could get boring at times. School would be back in session soon so I wasn't too worried about it.

I sent Pharaoh a text asking him was he too busy to pick me up. I thought about the conversation we had earlier and it was really time for me to get a car. I added getting my permit to my list of things I had to do. I started cleaning up my area because when it was time to leave I wanted to be the first person out the door. It was almost time for all of us to leave when my mother walked in. She looked a lot better from the last time I seen her.

"Aria, what are you doing here?" I asked her.

"I came to talk to you."

"Talk about what? And how did you know where I work?"

"Is there somewhere we can talk in private?" she asked, looking around at everyone in the salon.

"Yea follow me."

A million things were going through my mind, but one thing I already had in my head was that if my mother tried anything I was going to kick her ass right out. I opened the door to the office and Paige's head popped right up.

"Mom!" she yelled, coming from behind the desk and giving Aria a hug.

"Paige I missed you so much," Aria said. I didn't know if the words were genuine or not, but I knew hearing them would make Paige happy.

"I missed you too! Me and Royal went to go see you the other day but the man said you wasn't home."

"Yea mommy has been trying to get herself better so I can take you home with me."

"Paige go sit with Emerie while I talk to ma," I said, feeling the need to step in. As far as I was concerned, Paige wasn't going home with anyone but me. I didn't give a fuck if my mom went to rehab or not. Paige gave my mother one more hug before going out the room. Once she was gone, I shut the door behind her and went to sit in the chair behind the desk. I motioned for my mom to have a seat. I stared at her while she looked around the office, avoiding eye contact. The fact that she wouldn't look me in the eye had me feeling a little odd about this whole thing.

"Aria what did you want to talk about?" I asked her, breaking our silence.

"How many times do I have to tell you that I am your mother and you will respect me?"

"What did I say that was so disrespectful?" I asked, really wanting to know.

"You calling me by my first name is disrespectful. How would you feel if your kids called you by your first name?"

"First off my kids would never call me by my first name because they would know that I am their mother. They would know what it feels like to have a mother around. You say I'm disrespecting you by calling you Aria, but you haven't showed me anything else. I don't know you as my mother because you were never around."

"You're right Royal, I never was around but I'm trying to change that. You told me to get myself together and I did that. I just want to be a part of you and Paige's life. Paige is still young, I have time to make things right with her. But the real question is, do I have time to make things up with you?" she asked, with fake tears rolling down her face. I didn't know if the tears were fake or not, but I didn't put anything past her.

"Honestly speaking, there is nothing you could really do to change my mind about you. I'm already grown and taking care of myself. There is nothing to make up, I'm past it and I accepted it for what it was. Paige is a different story, she is young and doesn't know what is going on. If you are clean like you say you are I'll allow you to be a part of her life, but as soon as you fuck up I promise you that you will never see her again."

"I'm not going to fuck up I promise. I guess we can leave from here to pick up Paige's stuff so she can come home with me," Aria had the nerve to say.

"Paige isn't going anywhere with you. You will have supervised visits until I feel comfortable with the idea of you being around Paige."

"How are you going to dictate when I am going to see my daughter?"

"I have been taking care of your daughter for as long as I can remember, therefore she is my daughter and I will say when and where you can see her. Now if you don't mind, the shop is closing," I said, getting up.

I opened the door for her and watched her walk out with a stank attitude. She gave Paige a kiss before she walked out the door. I didn't care about her having an attitude, she was lucky I was even agreeing to let her be around Paige. Everyone cleaned up the shop and we all said our goodbye's after locking up. I was about to call a cab when Pharaoh pulled up in front of me.

"Why didn't you text me back letting me know you were coming?" I asked, strapping Paige into the backseat.

"I could have sworn I did, but hurry up Slim, I have to drop you off then go over to my crib and pick up some shit so I can handle that business later."

"Okay, Okay," I said, getting in the car.

He must have really been in a hurry because the drive from the salon to my house usually took forty- five minutes; this nigga cut the drive in half. He pulled up, helped me bring Paige in the house and was gone. This would be the first night I would be home while he was out handling business. To say I was worried was an understatement. I prayed he would come back to me safe and sound.

Pushing all thoughts of Pharaoh to the side, I made Paige her dinner and cleaned up a bit. After she ate, I sent her to take a bath and once she was done I told her she could watch TV for an hour. I finished cleaning and went to my room to change into my PJ's. Walking out my room to go brush my teeth, I peeked in Paige's room and she was knocked out. I went in, turned off the TV, kissed her on the forehead and told her I loved her. While I was headed back to the bathroom I heard my phone ring. I ran to go get it, thinking it could be Pharaoh.

"Hello," I answered, out of breath.

"Damn ma, you running a marathon over there?" I looked at my phone's screen because I didn't recognize the voice. The number on the screen was one I didn't recognize so I hung up the phone.

Two seconds later, my phone rang again and it was the same number. I let it ring out thinking the person who was calling would get the hint. They obviously didn't because they kept calling back.

"Hello?" I snapped, letting the caller know I had an attitude.

"First time you get on the phone you out of breath and now you get on the phone and you got an attitude," the person said laughing.

"It doesn't matter how I answered the phone, what matters is who is playing on my phone."

"Ma you forgot about me already? It's Zalen."

Zalen? How the hell did he get my number because I didn't remember giving it to him.

"Ohhh Zalen," I said, giggling a little. "How did you get my number?"

"After you left I went back over to Justice's crib and got the number from her, I hope its 'ight me calling you."

"It's cool, but ummm, let me call you back though," I said, hanging up before he even had a chance to respond.

I needed to call Justice because I didn't appreciate the fact that she gave this dude my number when she knows I'm fucking with Pharaoh.

"Why you giving niggas my number?" I asked, not giving her the chance to say hello.

"Well hello to you too hoe, and what niggas am I giving your number to?"

"Zalen!"

"You acting like I gave your number to twenty- five dudes!"

"That's not the point. Why would you give my number to any dude when you know I'm dating Pharaoh?"

"Okay you're *dating* Pharaoh, not marrying the nigga. Every dude has a side chick so why can't a female have a side nigga?" I looked at my phone to make sure I dialed Justice's number because the dumb shit that just came out her mouth had me thinking I called someone else.

"You sound dumb as shit. Look, please don't give anyone else my number please."

"Why not Royal, because you're too good for any of the niggas I fuck with?"

"Justice what are you talking about?" I was truly confused because she flipped the whole script.

"I'm so tired of you Royal," she said, slurring her words. At that point I knew she was drunk and some shit was about to start.

"You need to sleep off whatever it is you're drinking."

"I'm not drinking anything, I'm just keeping it a buck. You think you're above me and can talk to me any kind of way but guess what, you can't. You ain't shit but a nasty ass stripper that lucked up and snagged a nigga that is getting it."

"Justice I don't know what your problem is, but keep talking and you're not going to have a best friend anymore."

"Bitch I don't give a fuckkkkk! Shit, if I won't have a best friend anymore that means Pharaoh's fine ass is no longer off limits."

"Justice, Pharaoh wouldn't fuck with you if you were the last bitch on earth," I said, trying to hide how I really felt. I didn't know where all this was coming from but it was hurting me like hell.

"Yea 'ight Royal, you so naïve. Don't be mad when your nigga slip up and call you by my name," she laughed and hung up the phone.

I didn't know what had gotten into her but that's not how I pictured that conversation going. A part of me wanted to believe that Justice would never go that low and try to fuck with Pharaoh behind my back. But there was something telling me that this wasn't like any of our other fights. This fight felt like it was the end of our friendship and I had been told a drunken mind speaks sober thoughts.

Looking at the time and seeing how late it was I decided to go to bed and forget about the whole thing. If Justice wanted to act like a bitch then that was on her and I wasn't going to try to fix things later on. I thought about telling Pharaoh to watch out for Justice but at the same time, I didn't want to tell him because I wanted to see if he would fall for it. I made up my mind to just wait and see what happened. If Pharaoh did end up fucking with Justice behind my back then I knew my friendship with Justice would be truly over, and whatever Pharaoh and me had was straight bullshit.

Chapter 10

I woke up the next morning to my phone ringing off the hook. I looked at the time and it was only ten.

"Hello," I answered groggily into the phone.

"I didn't mean to wake you up ma," The person on the line said.

"Zalen?"

"That's twice in less than 24 hours that you forgot about me."

"It's not that I forgot about you, it's just too early in the morning, but wassup?"

"I was calling to see if I could take you to breakfast."

"I don't think so," I said, trying not to be rude.

"Why not Royal? I'm not gonna bite you ma," he said, laughing a little too much.

I got out of bed and went into the kitchen while he damn near begged me to go to breakfast with him. While I was getting a cup of water Pharaoh walked in carrying Paige. I gave him a strange look and he mouthed he will explain later.

"Royal you still there?" Zalen asked.

"Yea I'm here and I can't go to breakfast with you, I'm sorry."

"It's cool ma," he said and hung up.

I felt bad for turning him down but he came at the wrong time. If I didn't have Pharaoh in my life and he wanted to take me out maybe I would have went, but as for right now I had my hands full.

"Who was that on the phone?" Pharaoh asked, walking back in the kitchen.

"No one really. Why did you come in here carrying Paige?" I didn't like him taking Paige out the house without me knowing, especially since this was the first time he has ever done it.

"Instead of going home like I told you I was going to do I came here and slept on the couch. Paige woke me up early this morning saying she was hungry, so I took her to get some breakfast. It's no big deal Slim,." he explained and shrugged his shoulders.

"It is a big deal because if I would have walked in her room and she wasn't there I would've been ready to kill my mother."

"Your mother? Why would you think your mother had her?"

"Cause she came to the shop yesterday talking about how she went to rehab for her drinking and that she wants to make things right with me and Paige. I told her that whatever relationship we had is over but that she could spend time with Paige, just not alone. I don't trust her enough to leave her alone with Paige."

"Your mom is a trip and you know I wouldn't do anything to hurt Paige, plus I left you a note on the fridge saying where we were going. If your ass wasn't all into your phone call you would have seen it," he said, taking the note off the fridge and throwing it at me.

"Don't throw stuff at me and I wasn't all caught up in my phone call. I just had a real stressful night," I said, only telling him half the truth.

"Don't let that shit with your mom stress you Slim, just continue to focus on doing what you been doing."

"I know I shouldn't let her stress me. I don't want her coming back then when Paige gets use to her being around she just ups and leaves."

"If she does that I promise to put a hot one in her," he said, coming over and kissing me. The way his lips lingered against mine had me wanting to do some things.

"You better stop before you start something," I said, biting on his lip.

"Nah Royal, you better stop before I put something in you," he whispered in my ear.

I watched him as he walked towards the bedroom. I wanted to follow right behind his ass. Instead, I had to start getting ready for work, but first I wanted to talk to Paige about our mother. Walking into her room, she was laying on her bed watching TV. Paige was really a good kid and I didn't want my mother fucking that up.

"Did you have fun at breakfast with Pharaoh?" I asked her, jumping on her bed.

"Yea I like him. Are you gonna marry Pharaoh?" she asked, looking at me with hopeful eyes.

"I'm not sure. Only he knows that."

"I think you should."

"Maybe I will but I want to talk to you about mom."

"Are we gonna go see her?"

"Not today but we are going to see her soon."

"Yayyy I can't wait," she said smiling.

"I know you miss her Paige, but you have to understand that you won't be able to see her every day."

"I understand Royal, are we going back home?"

"This is our home."

"Our other home silly!" she laughed.

"No we won't, this is our new home from now on, okay?"

"Okay Royal."

"Now what are you going to do today? You want to come with me to work?"

"Nope I'm hanging with Pharaoh today."

"You are?"

"Yup, he said he will take me to Toys R Us."

"Make sure you pick something up for me okay?"

"You're too big for toys Royal."

"No I'm not," I said, acting like I was pouting.

"Okay, Okay, I'll get you something," she laughed, hugging me.

"Thank you, now let me go get ready for work. I'll see you later, okay?"

"Okay I love you."

"I love you too." I kissed her on the forehead and went into my room to find something to wear and to get in the shower.

I wasn't really in the mood to go to work, I just wanted to have a day for myself. I stripped out of my clothes and put on one of my robes. Pharaoh wasn't in the room anymore, but I had a good guess on where he was. I knocked on the bathroom door because when I tried to turn the knob it was locked.

"Who is it?" he yelled out.

"Open the door and find out," I said seductively.

I heard the door unlock, but still he didn't open the door. I pushed the door open, pulled the shower curtain back and dropped my robe.

"Royal what are you doing?" he asked, eyeing my body with lust. He must have thought I was playing when I told him he was gonna start something.

"What do you think I'm doing?" I said, getting in the shower. I stood right underneath the showerhead with my head tilted back letting the water run all over my body. The way Pharaoh was biting his lip I knew he was enjoying the show. I started rubbing my nipples making them stand at attention. Looking down at Pharaoh, his dick was rock hard and I had this urge to wrap my lips around it. The shower wasn't that big but there was still some space between us. I walked closer to him, pressing my body against his and started nibbling on his ear.

"Ahhh," he moaned in a husky voice.

"You wanna see what my mouth do?" I whispered in his ear. The question was rhetorical because whether he wanted me to show him or not I was going to.

I made a trail with my tongue starting from his ear and stopping once I was face to face with my new best friend. I let my tongue circle around his tip while I stroked him up and down. I licked the whole shaft before I made it disappear in my mouth. Every time I would deep throat his dick, I would hold his balls up and lick them before slowly releasing his dick from my mouth. Pharaoh had his head tilted back with both hands on my head. He started pumping his pelvis, fucking my mouth. I started playing in my own wetness and was ready to feel him inside of me. I stopped Pharaoh from moving and lifted his dick so it was resting on his stomach. Starting at his balls and going all the way up to the tip I snaked my tongue in a figure eight motion.

"Oh shit Slim," he moaned.

I did it a couple more times while I fingered myself. I took the juices that were on my finger, stood up and put both my fingers in Pharaoh's mouth.

"Mhmmm," he said, licking everything off them.

Looking in his eyes, you could tell there was only one thing on his mind. I'm sure looking in mine you could see the same thing. He turned me around and pushed me up against the wall. I poked my butt out so he wouldn't have any problems getting in. He grabbed my hair, making me tilt my head back and slapped my ass.

"You like this rough shit don't you?," he whispered, rubbing my ass.

"Yess Daddy!" I hissed.

He didn't even give me a warning, he just rammed all ten inches of thickness inside of me. I was trying not to moan too loud because Paige was in the house and these walls were paper thin, but Pharaoh was giving me the business.

"Shhhh," he said, biting my hair.

I threw my ass back, bringing us both more pleasure. I was on the verge of cumming but I didn't want it to end. The way he was making me feel was how I wanted to feel all day. As much as I wanted to hold off cumming, I couldn't help it. I let it all go and my body got weak to the point I almost fell.

"Nah you aint getting away that easy. You wanted to start some shit so let a nigga finish it," Pharaoh demanded, catching me.

He turned me around so I was facing him and wrapped one of my legs around his waist. He put his dick back in and I almost fainted. He was pumping in and out of me and hitting my g-spot at such a fast pace, that within seconds I was cumming again.

"Slim?"

"Yea?" I answered, barely able to form the word.

"I just need one more ma."

"One more? I was surprised I was able to do it twice."

"I got you Royal," he mumbled, shoving his tongue down my throat.

Unlike the other times he started going slow, making sure I felt everything. He wasn't fucking me anymore, it felt like it was so much more than that. My body and his were moving as one. I started scratching the shit out of his back because that was the only way I could express how I felt. As bad as I wanted to moan nothing would come out my mouth.

"Royal you gonna cum again for me ma?" Pharaoh asked in a sensual deep voice.

"Yesssssssss," I sang out while cumming.

"Royal I love you ma," he said. His body started tensing up, letting me know that he did what he said he was going to do; he put something in me.

He rested his body against mine as I rested mine against the shower wall. Nothing needed to be said in this moment because it was just that beautiful. I might not have told him that I loved him, but I'm sure he knew after what we just did.

******

"Royal why don't you take a day off for yourself and go chill with your friends?" Pharaoh suggested as we got dressed.

"I have to go to work. You know bills don't pay themselves."

"Don't worry I'll pay you for the day."

"Nah, I rather go to work. Paige told me you're taking her out today."

"Yea I don't really spend a lot of time with baby sis."

"Where are y'all going?"

"Stop trying to be nosey 'ight. I already told my mom you weren't going in to work so go have fun," he said, kissing me on the forehead and leaving out the door.

Since I wasn't talking to Justice, I didn't have any other friends I could chill with. I heard the front door close which meant Pharaoh and Paige were gone. I finished getting dressed and picked up the phone to call Emerie. Other than Justice, she was the only other person I really talked to.

"Hello?" she said, answering the phone.

"Em you at work today?" I asked, praying she said no.

"Nah I'm off, why wassup?"

"Pharaoh told me to take the day off and I don't have shit to do."

"I don't have anything to do either. Let's go to the mall, I need to go spend some money."

"I'm down. I have to go school shopping for Paige anyway."

"It's only the first week of August though," Emerie said laughing.

"I have to get a head start, plus I like to do everything early so I'm not rushing to do the shit last minute."

"I hear that because I do everything last minute. You have a ride or you want me to come pick you up?"

"Pharaoh left with Paige, so you can come get me."

"Ight, just text me your address and I'll be there in an hour or so."

"Ight," I said and hung up the phone.

I sent Emerie my address and went in the kitchen to get a bagel since I had time to kill until she got here. While eating my bagel I thought about Zalen. I really felt bad about the way I acted towards him. It wasn't that I didn't wanna be cool with him or anything, he just always called at the wrong time. I picked up my phone and decided to give him a call. I didn't think Pharaoh would mind because there was nothing going on between Zalen and me. He would just be a friend and that is all he would ever be.

"Yooo," Zalen said, answering the phone.

"That's how your mom taught you to answer the phone?" I said, laughing.

"Nah, but wassup what you want?"

"I was just calling to say sorry for how I've acted the last two times you reached out to me. But forget it because it sounds like you got an attitude." I didn't think he had anything to be upset about honestly. What nigga gets upset because a chick doesn't wanna talk to him? But then again in this generation, it was something that happened too often.

"Ight cool," he said and hung up.

I looked at my phone and started laughing because this nigga was really acting like a little bitch. Oh well, I guess I dodged a bullet from him. Looking back now I couldn't believe I had a crush on him. I turned the TV on when I got a text from Emerie saying she would be there in five minutes. I got up, grabbed all my things and went to meet her outside. That five minutes turned into ten. I was about to go back inside when I saw her black Mercedes coming down the block.

"What happened to five minutes?" I said, getting in.

"I didn't think the bridge was going to be that packed," she laughed.

"It's cool though."

"How's everything with you and Pharaoh?"

"It's cool, we taking it one day at a time you know."

"I can understand that, but you know that nigga loves you right?"

"How you know he loves me?"

"Anybody can tell. I have been working in that salon for about two years and he has never been around as much as he has since you started working there. Plus the way he looks at is like he only sees you and nobody else matters. When y'all get married I want to be a bridesmaid," she said, smiling.

"If we get married and I swear it's a big if, then you can be the maid of honor." I never really thought about marriage and it could be because I'm only 17, it just wasn't something that I put on my list of goals.

"Wait, I would've thought Justice would be your maid of honor," Emerie said, looking at me from the corner of her eye.

"Man I can't fuck with her! I don't know how our friendship started to go downhill, but she always saying some slick shit and giving dudes my number and I just don't want to deal with it."

"I can respect that, because her being your friend and knowing you got a dude she shouldn't be giving anyone your number. Bitches are so shady," she said, shaking her head.

I thought about telling her what Justice said about fucking with Pharaoh but I felt like I should keep that part to myself.

"Forget all of that, let's go shopping," I said and got out the car.

Walking into the mall it was beyond packed, there were people all over the place. We hit up Children's Place, The Gap, and Kids Footlocker for Paige. Once I felt like I got Paige everything she needed, Emerie and I circled back around the mall to go shopping for us. I was in such a good mood I even picked Pharaoh up a couple of things. We were in line at Macy's waiting for Emerie to pay for her stuff when I got a phone call. I had so many bags in my hand that I had to drop them all in order to answer my phone.

"Hello, hello?" I answered, hoping I caught the caller before they hung up.

"What are you doing Slim?" Pharaoh said laughing.

"At the mall with Emerie. Wassup? Is Paige okay?" I asked a little worried.

"Royal, Paige is fine. She's eating frozen yogurt right now."

"Oh okay, so wassup?"

"I was calling because I wanted to know if you were going to cook or not tonight."

"Yea I guess I can cook. You wanna come to my house or do you want me to go to yours?" I asked, trying to pick up my bags so we could leave.

"Come to mine, and my mom wants Paige to come over."

"I swear I never get to spend time with her anymore," I said, a little sad.

"Shut up Slim, you always with her," Pharaoh laughed at me.

"I guess she can go over there then."

"Ight, I'll drop her off before I come home."

"Okay tell her I love her."

"She said she loves you too and she got you a surprise."

"Tell her I can't wait to see it."

"Ight, I love you Royal," Pharaoh said, making me freeze up a little.

"Me too," I said quickly and hung up.

I was sure that's not what he wanted to hear me say but it was all I could give him right now. I just wasn't ready to tell him that I loved him.

"Royal you ready to go? I feel like I been in this mall forever," Emerie said.

"Yea but can you take me to the supermarket real quick? Pharaoh wants me to cook and I don't know what he got in his house."

"Sure no problem."

We headed out of the mall and walked over to the car. I put my stuff in the trunk so it would be easier for me to take it out when I got home. It didn't take long for us to get to the supermarket because there was one down the block from the mall.

"You don't have to get out, I'll be in and out," I told Emerie.

I walked in and went to the meat section first. Pharaoh didn't seem like a picky eater. I grabbed two chuck steaks so I could make pepper steak. I walked around the supermarket grabbing everything else I needed and walked out 10 minutes later. Walking to the car, I could see a guy leaning in the car window talking to Emerie. Getting closer to the car, I saw that it was Zalen. I rolled my eyes at him, walked right past him and asked Emerie to pop the trunk. After I put everything inside, I got in the car thinking Emerie would be ready to go but she was still talking to him.

"Royal this is my cousin Zalen, and Zalen this is my girl Royal," she said, thinking she was making an introduction. I couldn't believe this nigga was her cousin.

"We already know each other," Zalen said.

"Y'all do? How?" Emerie asked, looking between the both of us.

"We went to school together back in the day, it's nothing major," I said.

"She used to have a crush on me and now that I'm trying to get at her she acting like she don't want a nigga," Zalen said laughing.

"I tried to apologize for how I acted before but you were too caught up in your feelings. Oh, and I'm not acting like I don't want you, I really don't want you, but we can be friends though!" I said, laughing too.

"Boy you better leave her alone, she got a nigga," Emerie added.

"That don't mean anything, I don't see a ring," Zalen said, licking his lips.

"It might not mean anything to you but it means everything to me, now if you don't mind I would like to go home and cook for that man."

"The queen has spoken," Emerie laughed.

"That she has! I'll catch y'all later," Zalen said, winking at me.

"Be safe cuz," Emerie said and pulled out the parking lot.

"That boy is a trip," I smiled, shaking my head.

"Yea he is something else but he's a good dude."

I left the conversation at that because there was nothing else to say. He could be a good dude all he wanted to be, that didn't mean shit to me. Don't get me wrong, if I was still in high school I probably would have been all over him, but I was at a different place in my life and he just wasn't what I wanted.

Chapter 11

Emerie dropped me off 2 hours ago. When we pulled up to the house I saw Pharaoh's car parked in the drive way but he wasn't home. I put all of the stuff I bought from the mall up in the guest room and went back into the kitchen to cook.

While cooking I got a phone call. Thinking it was Pharaoh, I didn't bother looking at the caller id.

"Where are you?" I asked as soon as I picked up the phone.

"I'm where you're supposed to be," the voice said.

"Justice?"

"Damn you deleted my number that quick?" she laughed.

"What do you want because I don't got time for the games."

"I just wanted to tell you how good your nigga's dick tasted but you should already know that."

"What you are tasting is my juices bitch, I hope you love them shits too!" I said and hung up the phone. As soon as I hung up the phone with her, I called Pharaoh to see where he was. I'm sure he wasn't with Justice I had to call and make sure.

"Wassup Slim, you home?" he asked, answering the phone on the second ring.

"Yea I got here like two hours ago. I saw your car parked in the drive way but you wasn't in the house."

"Yea I dropped it off then got a ride with one of my boys. I had to do something real quick before I came home." I didn't want to not believe him, but it was kind of strange that one of his boys picked him up because I haven't met any of his boys.

"You dropped Paige off with your mother before or after you left your car here?"

"Yo Slim, what's up with all the questions?" he said, sounding defensive.

"Nothing, I just wanted to know if you had my sister out with you while you were handling business." I felt bad because I didn't have a reason to question him about anything. I was letting what Justice said get to me.

"I would never do anything like that Royal, but yo I'm like ten minutes away, I'll talk to you when I get there," he said and hung up the phone.

I threw my phone on the counter and finished cooking. I didn't know what type of mood I just put him in but I was hoping some food would calm him down. I shouldn't have even let what Justice said get to me. I needed to call Justice back to see what the real problem was because her coming at me came from left field. I finished making my dinner and washed all the dishes. Once I was done, I picked up my phone and called Justice.

"Let me guess, you called Pharaoh didn't you? You are so fucking gullible Royal," Justice snickered, not even letting the phone ring twice.

"Justice what's the problem for real? Why you mad at me? I have never done anything to you."

"You don't have to do anything to me for me not to wanna fuck with you anymore. You think because you're so perfect that everything revolves around you. We went out to the club and you left me to go be with Pharaoh."

"I didn't leave you, I went to go find you and because I did go looking for you, I had to beat Bia's ass."

"This is what I mean! How did we go from talking about me to us talking about you? You're just a selfish bitch!"

"Is the problem me being a selfish bitch, or is it because you're jealous of me," I asked, getting pissed off.

"Jealous of you for what Royal? Everything you got I can have and more," Justice said, sucking her teeth. I knew I hit a soft spot because whenever someone said something to her that hurt she would suck her teeth.

"I don't know what you are jealous of me for but it seems like you are. When I told you about my conversation with Pharaoh that night at the club, you had to throw shade and say he wasn't going to want me because I was a stripper. If that's not jealousy then I don't know what is."

"That's not jealousy stupid, that's stating the obvious," she said, laughing.

"Well it couldn't be too obvious because when the nigga found out he still wanted me."

"At least someone does because your mom damn sure doesn't."

At that point, I was ready to go over to her house and beat her ass. Even though I acted like I could care less about my mother, it took me a long time to get over that. Justice was the only person that knew how much I struggled with my mother neglecting me growing up. I didn't care if we were arguing or not, throwing that situation in the mix was a low blow and a deal maker.

"You know what Justice, I'm not even going to argue with you anymore because unlike you I'm not gonna hit you below the belt. You know how touchy the subject of my mother is but you still throw it in my face. Now that I think about it anything that was a touchy subject you threw in my face. I should have learned that night we went to the club that you wasn't my friend. But trust and believe I wasn't going to make that same mistake again. If I catch you in the street just know that it's on sight for you," I said, and hung up the phone.

"UGHHHHH!!!!!" I yelled just as Pharaoh was walking in the door.

"What are you yelling like that for?" he asked, coming into the kitchen and sitting down.

"Nothing, you ready to eat?" I asked, not really wanting to talk about what just happened. I didn't fully understand what happened so I damn sure didn't want to relive it.

"Yea, what you made."

"Pepper steak, rice and beans with corn on the cob."

"Yea I can fuck with that. Hopefully it will be as good as your breakfast," he laughed.

"What's that supposed to mean?"

"Some chicks can only cook breakfast," he said shrugging.

"Well this chick can cook breakfast, lunch and dinner. If you're good, I can even cook you dessert."

"Speaking of dessert, that shit you was doing in the shower surprised me Slim."

"Why were you so surprised?" I sat his plate in front of him and went to the fridge to get him a can of soda.

"Cause you only been with one nigga right?"

"Yea. So?" I said, not understanding what the problem was.

"If you only been with one nigga and once he hit it he left, how you learn how to do that shit you did in the shower?" he asked, putting a fork full of food in his mouth.

"So are you asking me how did I learn my tricks?"

"If you wanna share its cool, if you don't that's cool too."

"Then I choose not to share." I wasn't going to embarrass myself and tell him that I have been watching porn to learn certain things. Justice always told me I would have to learn how to hold my own in the bedroom.

I sat down and ate my plate of food with him. We were having a very casual conversation until Pharaoh pulled a box from out of his pocket. I didn't want to assume it was a ring but if it was one, I had to find a way to turn him down because I wasn't ready to be anyone's wife.

"Royal don't act like you don't see that box sitting there," he said, grabbing our plates and putting them in the sink. He sat back down and watched me watch the box.

"I see it, I'm just not sure I want to know what it is," I said nervously. If this was an engagement ring, I would have to disappoint him again. If I couldn't tell him that I loved him, how was I going to marry him? I prayed that Pharaoh was smarter than that.

"What you scared for? You probably thinking it's an engagement ring, huh?" he laughed.

"Why is that so funny though?"

"Why would I ask your ass to marry me when you can't even express your feelings to me? Come on Royal, ya boy ain't dumb."

"I'm glad you're not," I said, giggling a little. "If it's not an engagement ring then what is it?"

"Open it and find out."

I opened the box and it was a gold locket shaped like a crown. I opened it up and it had a picture of Paige and me. I wanted to cry because it was so beautiful; I jumped out of my chair and went to give Pharaoh a hug.

"Stop crying you cry baby," he said, kissing my forehead.

"This means everything to me Pharaoh, you just don't understand."

"Paige told me how your moms got her a gold locket and how she wanted you to have one too."

"My mom didn't get that for her, I did," I said sniffling.

"I figured that, but Paige picked out the picture and the locket, I just paid for it."

"Still, thank you so much Pharaoh. I swear that since you came into my life everything has gotten better. If it wasn't for you I probably would still be shaking my ass and struggling to take care of Paige."

"Don't thank me Royal. Everything that has been happening lately is because you had a determination to get your life back on track. All I did was offer you a job, the rest was all you," he said, kissing me.

Looking into his eyes, I couldn't deny that I loved him. The feelings I had for Pharaoh were unexplainable. He accepted me at my lowest point and not once passed judgment on me.

"I love you Pharaoh," I said, looking straight into his eyes.

"Don't just say it because you are caught up in the moment."

"I'm not caught up in the moment. I'm serious Pharaoh. I love you."

"Yea right, why you playing with a nigga?"

"I'm not playing, I'm so serious right now. I love you Pharaoh King," I said again, leaning in for a kiss.

This kiss felt different from all the other kisses we had. When our lips touched, I felt something electrifying.

"I love you too Royal King," he said.

"My last name is Preston, not King."

"It may be Preston now but it won't be for long," he said, carrying me up to the bedroom.

That night we made love until early in the morning. I gave him my mind, body and soul, and in return, he promised to love me, protect me and be honest with me. This is all I ever wanted out of a relationship, and for Pharaoh to give it me meant the world to me. I was riding with Pharaoh until the wheels fell off.

Chapter 12

Woke up sore as hell from the night before. I stretched and tried to get up but Pharaoh grabbed me and pulled me back down.

"Pharaoh come on, I have to get ready for work."

"You don't have to work, I'll take care of you Slim."

"Now you know that's not even gonna happen, now let me get up and get ready"

"I can't stand your independent ass," he said, letting me go.

"Yea right, you know me being independent is one of the reasons you love me," I told him and blew him a kiss.

I strolled in the bathroom and washed my face and brushed my teeth. I was about to get in the shower but Pharaoh's yelling stopped me. I walked out the bathroom to see him sitting up in the bed clenching his fists.

"Ight, good looks I'm on my way," he said and hung up the phone.

"Who was that? What's wrong?"

"Someone trashed mom's shop," Pharaoh said, getting up and gathering his clothes.

"Who was that on the phone, the police?"

"Nah it was Bia."

"Bia huh," I said, sucking my teeth.

"Yo Slim, now is not the time for your childish bullshit," he snapped, storming past me with a handful of clothes.

I thought it was funny that Bia called him saying the salon was trashed. Shit it was probably Bia's ass that did it. The more I thought about it, Justice could have easily done the shit too. I searched through my dressers for a pair of shorts and a baby doll t-shirt. I put on my Gamma 11's, put my hair up in a ponytail and was ready to go.

"Where the hell you think you going?," Pharaoh asked, coming out the bathroom.

"With you, duh."

"Look you don't have to come, nothing is going to happen between me and Bia ight."

"I'm not going because of Bia's ass, I'm going to be there for you. Now let's go before Bia talks to anyone else," I said and walked out the room.

We walked out the house at 11:00 and pulled up in front of the salon at 11:30. Bia was out front talking to the police and from the looks of it she was putting on a hell of a show. We got out the car and walked up, catching the end of the conversation.

"I don't know anyone who would want to do this," Bia said, shaking her head.

"Hey officers I'm Pharaoh King, I own the place," he said, shaking the cops' hands.

"Bia come walk with me so we can check out all the damage," I suggested, trying to give Pharaoh a minute to talk to the cops.

"I already checked it out, but you are more than welcome to go look while we finish the conversation. No disrespect Royal, but Pharaoh is the owner and I'm the one to find the place like this so I think I should stay."

"Nah it's cool you can go Bia. I'm sure you said more than enough," Pharaoh told her, shutting her ass up.

"Are you sure you don't need me?" she asked, caressing Pharaoh's arm.

I swear if these cops weren't here I would have beat her ass, I was starting to think she liked getting her ass beat.

"Bia if I need you I will let you know. Officers, come with me over here please," Pharaoh said, leading the officers away.

"Bia, why do you have to be so thirsty?" I asked, looking at her side ways.

"What, you can't handle a little competition?"

"What competition? You and I aren't even in the same lane."

"I know we're not because you could never compare to me. You think you have Pharaoh, well your wrong. You are just something for him to play with. Do you really think he will settle down with a 17-year-old?"

"Bia you are really sad. You're older than I am but you definitely act younger. You just can't come to terms that a chick younger then you took your man from you. You're mad because I'm everything you want to be and more. As far as me being compared to you I wish that never happens because then everyone will see in you what I see."

"And what is that?" she said, folding her arms.

"A failure that desperately needs a man to give her some type of purpose in life," I said and walked away. I didn't walk away with my back towards her this time. She had caught me slipping way too many times. This time I walked away facing her. I could see the anger, hurt and jealousy all in her eyes but I didn't give a fuck.

I looked around the shop and somebody did a number in here. The glass was broken on all the mirrors and everything that was in the stations was all over the floor. But what caught my attention the most was the spray paint on the walls. There weren't any words or anything, but there was spray paint all over the walls. It was interesting to me because usually when a person uses spray paint they want to draw or write something but I guess whoever did this had a different idea.

I walked out of the shop shaking my head because it would be a while before that place was up and running again, which meant I was out of a job for the time being. I looked around for Pharaoh because I was more than ready to go home.

"Pharaoh you ready to go?" I asked, walking up to him.

"Yea come on," he sighed.

He grabbed my hand and we walked over to the car. Before he got in, he looked back at the salon and shook his head. I think this was one of the only times I saw him this sad.

"It's going to be okay Pharaoh," I said, rubbing his back.

"I know it will. I'm not tripping off this," he said, pulling off.

"Then why you look stressed?"

"Because I need to find out who did this and I don't want them cops looking into my background. I always make sure to clean up my dirt but you never know though and those cops didn't look like they believed what I was saying."

"Is there anything I can do?" I offered, truly wanting to help.

"Look at you trying to be a ride or die bitch. But nah, there isn't anything you can do but keep your pretty ass by my side."

"You know I got you," I smiled.

"I know, but what were you and Bia talking about? I saw y'all over there and it was looking kind of intense."

"Nothing really, Bia was just being Bia," I said laughing.

"It couldn't have been too bad because I didn't have to pull you off of her."

"Not funny, but I'm tired of fighting her. Next time she gets disrespectful I'ma bust a cap in her ass," I said pointing my fingers like they were a gun.

"Royal do you even know how to shoot a gun?"

"Nope, but I can learn. All you have to do is aim and pull the trigger, it can't be that hard."

"Yea 'ight, I know never to leave a gun around your ass."

"Whatever, are we picking up Paige today?"

"It's up to you, when I called my moms earlier to tell her about the salon she said you don't have to be in a rush to get Paige."

"I know your mom likes spending time with her but I was thinking maybe we could pick her up and let her spend some time with my mom."

"It's whatever you want to do Royal, you know I got you."

"Ok let me call my mom and see if she wants to meet us at the Brooklyn Zoo."

I called my mom and she answered right away. We had a brief conversation before I told her about meeting us at the zoo. She said she would love to go and she would meet us there soon. I hung up the phone thinking that things would be different this time.

"What she say?" Pharaoh asked.

"She gonna meet us there in like an hour."

"Ight, let's go get baby sis then we can be out."

I nodded my head in agreement, sat back and enjoyed the ride. I wasn't too happy about seeing my mother but I knew Paige would be thrilled.

******

"Mommy!" Paige shouted, running up to my mother.

"I missed you so much," she said, hugging Paige.

"I missed you too, did you miss Royal and Pharaoh too?"

"I missed Royal, I haven't met Pharaoh yet," she said, taking Paige by the hand and walking towards Pharaoh and me.

"Mommy, this is Pharaoh," Paige said, grabbing Pharaoh's hand.

"Ma, this is Pharaoh, Pharaoh this is my mother Aria," I said giving them a formal introduction.

"It's nice to meet you," Pharaoh smiled, showing off them dimples that I loved.

"It's nice to meet you too. I can see that you're a big part in my daughters' lives," my mom said, eyeing him up and down.

"I would like to think that I am but I think they are a bigger part in my life."

"As long as you treat them right you won't have a problem with me."

"I don't plan on doing anything other than treat them right."

My mom nodded her head and let Paige lead her around the Zoo. Pharaoh and I lingered behind them. I wanted to give them some type of privacy but I still wanted them to be in my sight.

"You know you would make a great mother right?" Pharaoh said, grabbing my hand as we walked.

"Where did that even come from?"

"I watch how you treat Paige and I was thinking about kids."

If we were going to have this conversation then I had to stop walking and five him my full attention.

"Why you stop walking?"

"I'm not sure if I want kids. I'm still a kid myself if you think about it."

"You don't want kids at all?" Pharaoh asked, looking a little hurt. I knew I had to choose my next words wisely because we had just gotten to a good place and I didn't want to mess things up.

"It's not that I don't want to have kids, I really haven't given it any thought. I'm only 17 and kids are the furthest thing from my mind."

"I get it, but you will have my babies."

"What you mean I'll have your babies? I'm not having nothing if I don't want to."

"Royal don't try to act tough with this 'ight."

"I'm not acting tough, I'm so serious right now."

"Royal shut up because for all you know you could be pregnant right now. We haven't used a condom since we first started fucking." Thinking about what he said, he was absolutely right.

"Nigga!!! Are you trying to trap me?" I asked, taking a few steps back from him.

"Me try to trap you? Funny. If you were to get pregnant with my baby trust me it wouldn't be entrapment," he smirked.

"You are so full of yourself," I said, shaking my head at him.

"You can be full of me too," he whispered in my ear.

"You're so nasty. Let's go find my mother and Paige," I said and walked off.

Walking around the zoo, we found my mother and Paige over by the gift shop. We walked up just as my mom was buying Paige a stuffed lion.

"Royal look what mom got me!"

"It's pretty, you almost ready to go?"

"I don't want to leave mommy," Paige pouted.

"I know, but we have to go and get something to eat."

"Can mommy come?"

"No honey, I have something I have to do, I'll see you soon I promise," My mother said, stepping in.

"Okay. I love you mommy," Paige said, hugging her.

"I love you too Paige. Royal I'll see you later," mom said and walked away. I kind of felt bad but I knew I was doing what was right. I took Paige's hand and we all walked to the car.

"Where are we going now Royal?" Paige asked from the backseat.

"Where ever you want to go."

"I wanna go back to Ms. Adira's house."

"Why are you always trying to leave me?" I turned around in my seat and made a sad face trying to make her feel bad for me.

"I'm not always leaving you."

"Yes you are, which is why you are coming home with me."

"Okay, Okay, can we watch movies and stuff?"

"Of course we can."

The rest of the day was spent in the house. We watched every movie Paige wanted to watch no matter how boring it was. We were in the middle of watching Frozen when I heard something shatter in the kitchen. Pharaoh and I jumped up and found the kitchen window busted and Justice standing outside laughing with a bat in hand.

"Yo Royal, what the fuck is this?"

"I don't know but I'm about to find out. Paige go to your room," I yelled.

I was pissed that she broke my window, but I was happy we decided to come here instead of Pharaoh's house because if I would have come home to this I would have been even more pissed. I ran upstairs, grabbed my sneakers and went outside. Pharaoh was right behind me even after I told him I didn't need his help.

"The queen couldn't come outside alone, she had to bring her nigga too. Matter of fact I'm glad you brought his fine ass so I can show him what a real bitch is."

"Justice what the fuck is wrong with you for real yo?!" I yelled at her, getting pissed off.

"Shut the fuck up!" Justice shrieked, swinging her bat towards me.

I don't know how, but Pharaoh grabbed the bat in midair and ripped it out of her hands.

"Aint none of that gonna be going on. I don't know what happened between the two of y'all but I'm going to go check on baby sis before I have to hurt someone," Pharaoh said, walking off and going inside with the bat.

"Damn I need a nigga like that!" Justice grinned, watching Pharaoh walk away.

"Too bad no nigga will ever want your hoe ass," I said, rolling my eyes at her.

"I may be a hoe because I sleep with dudes, but at least I didn't need a nigga to come and save me. If you didn't have Pharaoh you would still be shaking your ass for them old ass dudes and coming to my house crying to me. You're not shit Royal. Your name might be different, special and unique, but you not. You just a basic bum bitch."

At that moment I was seeing red. I didn't remember how it happened, but I ended up on top of Justice beating her ass. At that moment I wasn't only fighting Justice, I was fighting everyone who had ever did me wrong. It just so happened to be Justice that brought all this anger out of me.

"Yo, chill Royal!" I heard Pharaoh yell out.

"You telling me to chill when she came to my house disrespecting me!" I yelled, huffing and puffing.

Pharaoh carried me away from Justice and went to help her up. I could have sworn my eyes were playing tricks on me. I couldn't believe this nigga helped that bitch up.

"So this is what we doing now? You gonna help her up like she didn't deserve that ass beating?" I screamed ,screwing my face up.

"Slim chill. I don't know what's going on, all I seen was you on top of her."

"You so concerned about that bitch you can leave with that bitch," I said, walking in the house and slamming the door.

This nigga had me fucked up! I know he saw her try to hit me with a bat, but you are gonna tell me to chill because I beat her ass???? This nigga had me fucked all the way up! I was born and raised in Brooklyn, and one thing this Brooklyn bitch doesn't put up with is disrespect.

"Where is Pharaoh?" Paige asked, coming out the room.

"He's going home. Go back in your room until I'm done cooking dinner."

She looked like she had something else to say but the look on my face let her know I wasn't in the mood for any back talk. While she was walking towards her room, Pharaoh came walking in the house like I didn't just tell his ass to leave.

"I could have sworn I told your ass to leave," I said, walking in the kitchen.

"I'm not going anywhere until your stubborn ass talks to me."

"I don't want to talk to you, what part of that don't you understand my nigga?"

"Yo Royal, who you talking to like that? I'm not one of these little bitches that you be fighting in the streets," he said, getting in my face.

"Pharaoh you need to get out my face!" He must have thought I was playing but I was on ten right now and I didn't care if I couldn't beat his ass, I was more than ready to try at this moment.

He put one hand around my neck and shoved me against the wall. I didn't know what type of bitches he fucked with but I wasn't going to let him put hands on me. Since he wasn't holding my hands, I used my left hand to slap him.

"Ight, I give you that, you caught me slipping but I got something for your ass."

He pulled me forward by my shirt and shoved me back against the wall. He raised both my hands above my head and held them there with his right arm.

"You like this rough shit, don't you Royal?" he said, pointing his finger in my face.

"Fuck you and that bitch!" I yelled.

"You lucky I love your little ass because I'm not one for the disrespect."

"I don't care if you love me or not, I fucking hate you. Now let me go and get the fuck out of my house!"

"You hate me Royal?" he asked, kissing on my neck.

"Yea I fucking hate you and that dumb ass bitch," I said, trying not to moan. I don't know what Pharaoh thought he was doing, but he wasn't going to get any sex from me ever again.

"You can hate Justice all you want but your ass better not hate me or I'ma fuck you up," he said, letting me go. I watched him walk out my house and possibly out of my life for good.

I didn't feel like cooking anymore so I put some pizza rolls in the oven for Paige. It didn't take long for them to cook. When they were finished, I poured her some juice and took it to her room.

"Here you go. I'm going to go lay down in my room. If you need me just come get me, okay?"

"Are you okay?"

"Yea I'm fine, just a little tired," I answered, lying to her.

"Okay, go get some rest. I love you."

"I love you too Paige," I said and walked out the room.

I went in the kitchen and got the only bottle of wine that was in the house. I wasn't much of a drinker, but Pharaoh's mom got it for me as a house-warming present. With the way I was feeling I could use a drink or two. I went in my room, scrolled through my phone's music and went straight to my R&B playlist.

My heart was hurting and I didn't have anyone to talk to. I lost my best friend and boyfriend in the same night. Fuck Justice! I was hurt, but I would get over our situation sooner than later. But when Pharaoh picked her up off the ground, I swear my heart broke. I didn't care if he was trying to do the right thing, he was supposed to be on my side and being on my side consisted of him letting me beat her ass. The crazy thing is when he walked out the door I felt nothing. It was like my whole body went numb, but I knew him leaving was the best thing for us. There was no way that I could be with him after this. I downed about three cups of wine back to back. I was pouring another glass when my phone starting ringing.

"If I kicked you out my house what makes you think I want to talk to you on the phone," I said, thinking Pharaoh was on the phone.

"Damn, who broke your heart?" The person on the other side of the phone said.

"Don't worry about who broke my heart just tell me who this is." The wine had me buzzed and I really couldn't focus on anything.

"Zalen," he said, sounding frustrated.

"Ewww, why you sound like that? You called my phone and have the nerve to get an attitude with me."

"I'm not mad at you, it's cool ma. Have a good night," he said, and hung up the phone.

I didn't know what the hell was going on but it seemed like a lot of niggas were starting to act like bitches, and Pharaoh was one of them. I was so pissed off and hurt by him. For the rest of the night I stayed up drinking my bottle of wine and crying. At this moment, love didn't live here anymore and I didn't want anything to do with Pharaoh's dumbass.

Chapter 13

"Royal get up, Ms. Adira is here," Paige said, shaking me.

"Okay, okay," I groaned, trying to get out bed.

Paige had to help me stand up because as soon as I got off the bed I almost fell over. I grabbed my robe from off the back of the door and put it on.

"Hey Adira," I said, opening the door for her.

"Chile what happened to you? You look horrible," she said as she walked in. I felt like shit, leaving me to assume that I looked the same way, but there was no need to assume it because Adira already confirmed it.

"Nothing I just had a rough night."

"I can see that. Pharaoh told me what happened." As soon as she said Pharaoh told her I rolled my eyes because why did he always go and tell his mother everything?

"Don't roll your eyes at me young lady. Just because he told me what happened doesn't mean I agree with what he did."

"No disrespect, but I don't really want to talk about this right now," I said, holding my head, trying to stop it from spinning. From the way I felt you would have thought I drunk something harder than wine.

"I respect it. I just came over here to get Paige because I figured you could use some alone time.''

"That's fine, her room is straight to the back," I told her and leaned back on the couch.

I was grateful that Adira was taking Paige because I wasn't sure how I was going to make it through the day, let alone take care of Paige too.

"Alright I got all her stuff. Whenever you're ready to come get her just let me know and I'll drop her off to you."

"Okay and thank you. Paige behave, okay?" I told her.

"I always behave. Get better Royal," Paige said, waving as she walked out the house. I shut the door and went right back to bed. I didn't want to be bothered with anyone, shit I didn't even have anyone to be bothered with. Getting back in bed, I snuggled up to one of the extra pillows and went back to sleep.

******

I'll be back at 11, you just act like a peasant. Got a bow on my panties because my ass is a present. Yea, it's gooder than Meagan, you look good when you're beggin', I be laughing when you begging me to just put the head in. Let me sit on your face, it's okay you could play with. When I'm bouncing it chill out and don't you make a mistake with it. Let me see what you're working with, If I'm ridin', I'm murkin' it, slow grindin' I'm twerkin' it. Yea I bagged him I'm Birkin'd it.

My phone playing Nicki's new song, "Get On Your Knees" woke me up out of my sleep. I looked all over my bed for my phone but I couldn't find it. I gave up looking for it and figured if the phone call was important the person would leave a message.

I forced myself to get up and go into the bathroom. I looked in the mirror and I was disgusted with myself. All I saw was my mother's reflection. The way she would get up and act all sluggish was exactly how I was acting right now. I had to let Paige go with Pharaoh's mom because I didn't think I was going to be able to take care of her today. Shaking off my self-pity I pushed myself to get in the shower, hoping it would help me shake this hangover.

The water pouring over my head gave me flash backs of me and Pharaoh in the shower. Shaking Pharaoh was going to be a hard task to do, it was like everywhere I went something reminded me of him. I lathered up my loofa and washed, trying to wash all the memories away too. I dried off, wrapped a towel around me and got back in bed. The shower had me feeling a little bit better but I still didn't want to do anything other than sit in bed. When I went through my first heartbreak, I had Justice to help me get through everything. Now I didn't have anyone and as much as I wanted to act like I was tough right now, I felt more vulnerable than ever.

Just as I was dozing back off my phone started ringing again. I looked at the caller ID and it was Zalen. This was the most persistent nigga I have ever met. No matter how many times I igged his shit, he still called back.

"Hey Zalen, wassup?"

"I'm calling to say sorry for last night. I don't know what you're going through and I had no right to go off on you."

"It's cool," I said, keeping it short.

"No it's not okay, and I won't be calling you anymore. I should have learned my lesson the last couple of times."

"Nah it's cool, I should be apologizing because every time you call I act like a complete bitch."

"Don't worry about it, but I hope everything is okay with you."

"I'm doing alright."

"That's good. Just remember that things get greater. Ight? Later."

"Okay."

"Ight, bye Royal."

"Bye Zalen," I said and hung up the phone.

Getting that call from Zalen had me thinking about the crush I had on him in high school. The only reason I never really talked to him back then was because he was always into some shit. He was the type of dude that your parents would warn you to stay away from. But for some reason I was drawn to him. I couldn't help but think how life would be if I gave him a chance. He was still cute as hell and I'm sure the feelings were still there, but could I really just forget about Pharaoh and move on? I nixed the thought because I knew that how I felt about Pharaoh was a lot stronger then what I felt back then for Zalen. Even though Pharaoh and I were going through it right now, I wasn't sure if I was ready to walk away. One thing my mom did teach me was to never make decisions on temporary feelings.

Chapter 14

It has officially been a week since I talked to Pharaoh and it was killing me. The shop was still closed so I used my time to get my driver's permit. Paige was still staying with Adira but I would go and see her from time to time. When I did go see her she would make sure her son was nowhere around. Surprisingly, she has been very understanding and hasn't been trying to force me to talk to him.

Pharaoh on the other hand, has been calling me like crazy these last three days. After everything happened, he wasn't trying to get in touch with me at all. I guess he realized I was serious about things being over. My whole thing was that if he really wanted to see me all he had to do was come to my house because he still had a key and I didn't change the lock. I truly missed him, it was like a piece of my heart was missing without him.

While I was getting dressed so I could get my day started, I was playing, Rain by Razah. Not a lot of people knew about him but his music spoke to me, especially this song. This song has been on repeat for the past week. As the song started, I sang along word for word because this is how I truly felt.

Let the rain fall down, take me away cause' I don't wanna be without   *you.*
Boy I can't sleep without you here, so let the rain take me away.
When you left you took my heart from me you mean the world to me.

Every time I sang that part, I would break down and cry and this time was no different. I knew I had to go and talk to Pharaoh, because he meant the world to me and without him in my life, I just couldn't function. I called Emerie to see if she would give me a ride over to Pharaoh's house. She said she would and that she would be here in thirty minutes. I curled my hair and stood in front of the closet looking for something to wear. I needed to look my best to make it seem like being without Pharaoh didn't faze me this whole week. I decided on wearing a black dress that hugged my body perfectly and gold gladiator sandals. If I would have walked out the house in that I would look plain, and plain wasn't my style. I added some big gold bangles and the locket that Paige got for me with a gold body necklace. I gave myself the twice over and was more than pleased with my look. I sprayed my Warm & Comfy perfume and was ready to go.

I was anxious as hell waiting for Emerie to tell me she was outside. I figured to kill time I would check the mail. I took the mail out went back inside and started going through it. Most of it was junk mail until I got to a letter from Brooklyn College. I was nervous as hell because this is the letter I was waiting for. I opened and skimmed through the letter and almost fell out of my seat.

"Yesssss!!!!!" I yelled, happy that I had got in.

My day just kept getting better and better, and by the end of tonight I would have had the best day ever. My phone started vibrating so I took it out my pocket. It was a message from Emerie saying to be outside and that she was just up the block. I threw my acceptance letter into my purse and was out the door.

"Who are you trying to look all cute for?" Emerie asked when I got in the car.

"I plan on getting my boo back," I said smiling.

"Well before we head over there I have to make a detour."

"Where do you need to go?"

"So don't get mad at me okay?" she said, avoiding eye contact.

"What?" I knew it had to be something bad because Emerie was the type that would just tell it like it is.

"Bia called me early saying----"

"What the fuck is Bia's old ass calling you for?" I said, cutting her off.

"If you would have let me finish I would tell you."

I sucked my teeth and rolled my eyes at her. I just got some of the best news and I didn't really need Bia fucking it up.

"Go ahead," I told her.

"Like I was saying, Bia called me earlier saying she had something to tell you and asked me if I could get you to meet up with her."

"She didn't tell you what she had to say?"

"Nope, she just told me to bring you in front of the shop. When you called me earlier saying you needed a ride I had just hung up with Bia."

"Why didn't you tell me then?" I asked. I could feel myself starting to get pissed off but I was trying my hardest to stay calm and just hear what Bia had to say.

"I knew if I told you before your ass would have never agreed to come."

She was right about that because if I had known I would have called a damn cab. Since I was already in the car, I had no choice but to go along. The whole car ride to the shop a million things were going through my mind as I thought about what Bia had to tell me. When we pulled up, I damn near jumped out of the car while Emerie was parking.

"What could you possibly want?" I asked, walking up to Bia, getting right to the point.

"Look we are not going to have any issues right?" Emerie said, looking between the both of us.

"I came here on peaceful terms," Bia said.

"I didn't wanna come here at all but since I'm here, talk."

"Okay, I asked you here because I saw your friend going into Pharaoh's house."

"What friend are you talking about?" I asked, just to see if she was telling the truth. I already knew who she was talking about because I only had one friend.

"The one you brought to the shop that time and I was beating your ass and she helped Emerie get me off you," Bia said, smirking.

"Bitch don't get smart, because you have never beaten my ass. You might have caught me off guard a couple times but that's only because you're a pussy ass bitch," I said, ready to beat her ass for the third time.

"How did you see her go into Pharaoh's house?" Emerie asked.

"I was parked outside his house when I saw her pull up. He opened the door and let her in. That's when I called Emerie and I came straight here," she said as if it was perfectly fine.

"You need help because what the fuck are you doing sitting outside his house? Bitch, you aint his bitch!" I yelled, biting my lip to keep from smacking the shit out of her.

"Whatever. Call me what you want, but while you are here going off on me your friend is over there getting our dick."

Bia was really fucking crazy talking about "our dick". If it was one thing I didn't share, it was dick.

"I'ma let that last comment slide because you put me on. But if you are lying to me I promise that I will give you more than an ass beating," I said, then slapped her. "That's for saying 'our dick'. Bitch that was never your dick. Emerie let's go," I said and walked away.

I didn't know if Bia was telling the truth, but at the same time what reason did she have to lie? There was nothing for her to gain out of lying but I was on my way to find out.

"Why you slap that girl after you told her you let her slide with that last comment?" Emerie said, laughing her ass off.

"Because that bitch had the nerve to say 'our dick'. Like bitch, what? She never even had the dick."

"She is truly crazy, like why would she sit outside of his house though?"

"I don't know, but drive faster because I need to find out what the fuck is going on."

Emerie picked up the pace a little but I swear she still wasn't going fast enough for me. Everything that Justice had ever said to me about Pharaoh flashed through my mind and I was getting heated. If this bitch was really over there then it would be her last day breathing because both of them were going to die.

When Emerie pulled up to the house, my whole body got weak and I couldn't get out of the car. A part of me wanted to know if Justice was really there, but the other side didn't wanna believe that Pharaoh would play me like that.

"You want me to come with you?" Emerie asked.

"Nah, I just need a minute," I told her, trying to pull myself together.

"You sure you want to do this? It's going to hurt more if you catch them in the act Royal."

"I know, but I just can't end things with Pharaoh because of some shit Bia said. I have to see the shit for myself."

"I respect it, I just don't think you should walk into this alone."

"Don't worry about me Em, I'll be okay. Just be out here when I come out."

"Here, well take this with you since you don't know what you're walking into," Emerie said, handing me a .22"

I looked down, not really wanting to take the gun because I didn't think I had it in me to kill anyone.

"Just take it, you don't have to use it." I took the gun out her hand and got out the car.

The walk to his front door felt like the longest walk ever. I dug in my bag for the key. I tried to unlock the door but my hands kept shaking. I needed to take a minute to pull myself together. I had to walk in there ready to see the worse. Once I pulled myself together, I put the key in the door and walked in. Walking through the living room everything looked pretty normal, there wasn't anything out of place and it looked exactly as I remembered it. I walked up the stairs heading to the bedroom, making sure not to make any noise. When I got to the top of the stairs, I heard moaning coming from inside the master bedroom.

I wanted to break down and cry because the person moaning was a female and she sounded a lot like Justice. I slid down the wall and started crying my eyes out. I should have let Emerie come in with me because I was at a loss for words and felt like I couldn't breathe. The more I heard the female moaning the more my heart broke. At some point of me sitting there my hurt turned into pain. I looked down at the gun in my hand and took the safety off. I got up and wiped my eyes. Even though I was heartbroken, I wasn't going to let no nigga break me. I walked into the bedroom and saw Justice riding Pharaoh, reverse cowgirl.

"I told you I would get your man," Justice said when she saw me standing there. The look on her face was of pure pleasure. She didn't try to stop or cover herself up, she just kept riding Pharaoh with this devious smile as I stood there watching. I raised my gun and let off two shots. One hit her in her chest and the other in her stomach. She fell to the right instantly. I walked over to the side of the bed to look into Pharaoh's face.

"Royal?" he whispered.

"How could you do this to me?" I asked, crying. The look on Pharaoh's face showed pure confusion. He didn't look like he knew what was going on but the fact that his dick was hard let me know all I needed to know.

"I love you," I said as a tear slid down my face. I turned my head and fired two shot before running out of the room. I couldn't look at him while I killed him like I did Justice. I jumped in the car and told Emerie to drive.

"What happened?" she asked, looking at me but trying to keep her eye on the road.

"Justice was fucking Pharaoh," I said, putting my head down. The words sounded so funny coming out of my mouth.

"No way!" Emerie said.

"I'm so serious, and I killed them both," I said, shaking uncontrollable.

"You did what?" Emerie screamed, slamming on her breaks.

"I...I...ki...killed them," I said, forcing it out.

"Fuck!!!!!" she yelled, taking the gun out my hand and sitting it on her lap. "I gave you the gun to protect yourself not to fucking kill anyone!"

I couldn't respond because I couldn't believe I had just killed my best friend and the love of my life. How was I going to explain this to his mother? What if I go to jail? What's gonna happen to Paige? I guess Emerie realized I wasn't going to answer back because she picked up her phone and told someone to meet her at my house. What was normally a thirty-minute drive Emerie turned it into a ten-minute drive. Emerie helped me out the car and into the house. It was like I was in a daze. I sat on the couch trying to snap myself out of the trance.

Emerie kept walking around the house acting like that was going to change the fact that I just killed two people. About ten minutes of Emerie walking in circles there was a knock out the door. It must have been who she was on the phone with because she flew to the door. She walked back into the living room with Zalen and seeing him pulled me right out of that trance.

"What the fuck is he doing here? I don't need more people knowing what the fuck I did. Plus I don't trust his ass."

"Royal calm down, he is here to help us and he's my cousin so I trust him."

"He might be your cousin but he fucks with the dude that was fucking Justice."

"What is she talking about?" Emerie asked Zalen.

"She's talking about Raylon, he was sleeping with Justice," Zalen explained, taking a seat on the couch.

"He probably knew what the fuck Justice ass was up to," I said.

"I don't know what she was up to, I wasn't fucking her," he said.

"Ight everyone calm down, we have a problem and it needs to get fixed," Emerie said, trying to play the mediator.

"So what happened?" Zalen asked.

I wasn't going to say anything. I didn't feel like I could trust him.

"Royal tell him what happened so he can help you."

"I don't need him to help me, whatever comes of this I will deal with it."

"Royal stop acting like a dumb bitch. Did you forget that you have Paige to look after? What is she going to do if your ass ends up in jail?" Emerie yelled at me.

"Fine. I walked in the house, went upstairs, heard moaning, opened the bedroom door and saw Justice riding his dick in the reverse cowgirl position. She said some words, I said some words and then I shot her twice. I walked over to the side of the bed so I could see Pharaoh, turned my head and shot him twice and ran out," I said, crying all over again.

"Where is the gun?" Zalen asked.

"Here, I took it from her once she told me what happened," Emerie said, handing it to him.

"Who saw you walk into the house?"

"Just Emerie," I answered, and then something clicked.

"What happened, why are you looking like that?" Emerie asked me.

"Because you might have been the only person that saw me go in but Bia knew I was going over there."

"Oh shit," Emerie said, covering her mouth.

"Who's Bia?" Zalen asked with confusion all over his face.

"Bia is the chick that told me Justice was in Pharaoh's house," I explained, nervous as hell.

"Ight look, I'm gonna go get rid of the gun since it's the murder weapon. As far as Bia goes, it will be y'all word against hers. All y'all have to do is stick together and everything will be fine," Zalen said, getting up.

He gave both of us a hug and left out to get rid of the gun. I told Emerie she should stay at my house because it would look better for our alibi before I went upstairs. When I got to my room, I stripped out my clothes and got in the shower. I couldn't believe I had just committed a double homicide. My day started off so good and look how it was ending. The images of Pharaoh and Justice kept playing over and over in my head. The look on Pharaoh's face before I killed him had me puzzled. It looked like he was out of it, but I couldn't tell because the only thing that was on my mind was his dick being hard and Justice sitting on it. But what if Justice drugged him and took advantage of him? I shook that idea out my head because Justice was a little smaller than me, how could she drug Pharaoh's tall ass? I was coming up with excuses because I didn't wanna believe what I saw with my own two eyes.

I got out the shower and didn't even bother to dry off. I got right in bed and tried to go to sleep. But tonight I knew that sleep wasn't going to come easy. I was filled with guilt because of the crimes I just committed. Tonight was going to be the first night that was going to be filled with tears; I had 1 down and 364 more nights to go.

******

"Royal!!!!!!!!!!!" I heard Emerie yelling. I had just fallen asleep and now I had to be woken up. I looked at the clock over by my nightstand and it read 3:35 a.m. I got up slowly, grabbed my robe and went out to the living room.

"Emerie what do you want" I asked, rubbing my eyes. When my eyes were fully open I saw two officers standing at the door.

"Are you Royal Preston?" One of the officers asked.

"Uh yea, may I ask what's going on here?" I was putting up a strong front but I was scared as hell on the inside.

"Will you come with us downtown? We have a couple of questions that we need to ask you."

"Questions about what?"

"If you come with us we will be happy to answer any and every question that you may have."

"Just let me go put on some clothes," I said, turning to go back into my bedroom.

"I'm sorry but we can't let you do that," an officer said, walking up behind me with handcuffs in his hand.

"I thought you just wanted to talk to me? I didn't know I was going to get arrested," I said, trying to remain cool on the outside.

"Just come with us and we will explain everything." The officer put the handcuffs on me and lead me out the door.

"Don't worry I'm gonna be down there with some clothes for you and a lawyer," Emerie yelled out the door.

I didn't know what was about to happen but I knew that I had just gotten myself into some straight bullshit.

To Be Continued .....

Contact Me

Facebook: Kellz Kimberly

Instagram: Kellzkimberlyxoxo

Snapchat: Kellzkayy

Website: Kellzkinc.com

CPSIA information can be obtained
at www.ICGtesting.com
Printed in the USA
LVOW11s2047280318
571477LV00003B/557/P

9 781537 497365